Tales Of Sley House 2024

Edited by
Lillian Ehrhart

ISBN: 978-1-957941-12-7

Edited by Lillian Ehrhart
Book Cover by Ranxvrus

First Edition
2025

Contents

The Tales of Genevieve Sley

The Licker

Eric Raglin

Eric Raglin (he/him) is a queer Nebraskan horror/Weird fiction writer. His short story collections include Nightmare Yearnings, Extinction Hymns *(published by Brigids Gate Press), and* Lonesome Pyres *(forthcoming in 2024 through Off Limits Pulp). He owns Cursed Morsels Press and has edited* No Trouble at All *(with Alexis DuBon),* Bitter Apples, Shredded: A Sports and Fitness Body Horror Anthology, *and* Antifa Splatterpunk. *Find him on Twitter, Bluesky, or Instagram @ericraglin1992.*

ᘓᘔᘓᘔ

The Licker finally got me in the grocery store.

I was so focused on deciding between gummy worms and peach rings that I didn't hear him approach, but nobody ever does. I flinched when his tongue ran up my neck. It was wet and hot and rough, built for stripping the top layers of skin to dig up the richer flavor underneath.

Instead of fighting back or fleeing, I collapsed into the

candy display, plastic crinkling under my weight. My head was buried in sour Trollis, so I couldn't see The Licker's face, but nobody ever does. I just heard him gag and spit before he ran off.

This, more than the lick itself, haunted me.

❧

If it weren't for The Licker's disgusted reaction, I might have told my girlfriend about the encounter.

Julie had one of her own a few months back. While she was at the beach, half-asleep in the sun, The Licker snuck up, pressed his tongue to her foot, and moaned "mmmmmmm" like she was a prime cut of meat—her toes somehow tastier than my neck. By the time Julie sat up to smack him, he was already halfway to the water, his spindly humanoid form faster than any Olympian. He ran into the ocean, sank into the waves, and vanished.

Julie always told this story like The Licker's "mmmmmmm" was gross and awful, and I'm not saying it wasn't. I'm just saying his reaction to me was worse. After all, what could be more embarrassing—more hurtful—than a gag and spit? Like I was a turd on two legs. In all the time The Licker had been here— as far back as anyone could remember—no one had ever mentioned a reaction other than "mmmmmmm" or "yummmmmm" or "that's the stuff."

Why was I so different? What the Hell was wrong with me?

❧

Barely a week later, I convinced myself The Licker, like a dog, could detect cancer through his senses. Surely that was why he'd reacted to me with such disgust. No other explanation made sense. I'd always maintained good hygiene, scrubbing myself with apple-scented body wash each morning. Not only that, Julie eagerly licked and sucked me whenever we had sex.

So, I was dying. That had to be it.

I booked an appointment with a dermatologist, but she assured me my skin was fine: no strange cutaneous developments or suspicious moles. I insisted on a biopsy anyway.

"All healthy tissue, Mr. Crilly," she assured me over the phone a few days later. "No need to worry."

But how could I *not* worry?

I drove two hours outside of town to visit a more experienced doctor, but she also insisted I was healthy, if a bit on the anxious side. Her condescension poisoned the rest of my day.

Even if I didn't have cancer, something was still wrong with me.

Maybe The Licker had tasted my soul instead of my body. He wasn't quite human, after all, and no one in town truly understood his abilities or motivations. Maybe he was a perverse angel sent down to see which Hawley residents were fit for Heaven.

The more I considered the rot of my soul, the more it ate me up. I didn't mention these thoughts to Julie, but she could always tell when something was wrong.

One night in bed, she turned to me and asked, "What's going on, Alan? You've been out of it lately."

I considered telling her what happened in the grocery store, but I pictured her face contorting when I admitted to The Licker gagging and spitting. I pictured her whole image of me shifting in a split second, realizing The Licker had sensed something she'd missed: a massive red flag waving just outside her range of perception.

But I had to say *something*. If I brushed her off, she'd come to her own wrong conclusions—that I was cheating, for instance, or plotting suicide.

So instead, I asked, "Am I a good person?"

Julie gave me a concerned, cockeyed grin. "Yeah," she said. "Otherwise I wouldn't be with you. Why do you ask?"

"No reason. I'm just being hard on myself."

Julie squeezed my hand. "Listen. You helped my brother—the most obnoxious person in the fucking world—move into his new apartment. Would a bad person do that?"

"I guess not. I don't know."

Julie sat up and leaned in close. "I could keep listing good things you've done until you believe me."

"No, that's okay."

Julie looked like she wanted to ask more questions, but I turned out the nightstand lamp before she could.

Even with her reassurance, I barely slept. I stayed awake hoping to God she was right. If only I had the chance to make a better second impression. Maybe I could bring The Licker back to me.

⚬⚬⚬

The Licker rarely licked the same person twice, but it happened occasionally.

He'd first licked my friend Nate three years ago while he was bench-pressing at the gym, then again two months back while he was red-faced at the squat rack. A "yummmmm" had accompanied both licks. Anymore, Nate kept a taser clipped to his gym shorts in case The Licker came back for thirds.

Unlike Nate, I wanted The Licker to come back for me. I returned to the grocery store and pretended to browse the gummy candy selection, waiting. Maybe if he licked me again, my taste—physical or spiritual—would grow on him. Maybe he'd gotten me wrong the first time, and I was an acquired taste.

An hour passed, and still I waited.

"Sir, can I help you find anything?" a worker asked me, clearly unnerved by how long I'd lingered in the candy aisle.

"No, I just need a little more time," I said.

The worker gave a forced smile and walked away, her eyes darting back to me before she turned the corner. Maybe I'd be the weird customer she'd talk shit about with her friend over texts or her partner over dinner.

The thought was mortifying, but not enough to stop me. I had to keep trying. It didn't matter if no one else understood.

"Come back, Licker," I muttered, as if he could hear me from wherever he was—Heaven, Hell, the bottom of the ocean. "Please, just one more lick. Just one more…"

Three hours in, a cop came to deal with me.

"What's his problem?" he asked the worker who'd called him.

"He must be on drugs," the worker said. "He's just been standing there, talking to himself. It's creepy."

"Yeah, probably fucked up on something." He approached me from behind. "Sir, can you come with me?"

When the cop placed his hand on my shoulder, I shrugged him off.

"Give me a few more minutes," I said, an edge creeping into my voice.

When the cop puffed out his chest, I knew what kind of asshole I was dealing with.

"Sir," he said, "when an officer tells you to do something, you do it."

Again, he put his hand on my shoulder, but this time he clamped down. I tried to wriggle away, to pry his fingers loose, to buy myself a little more time. I couldn't give up so easily.

But a tight pair of handcuffs soon ended my struggle.

The cop could lock me in a cell if he wanted. The Licker

would still find me. I'd keep waiting, keep calling for him.

⚜

I sat in my cell, waiting for either The Licker to slip between the bars or a confused, pissed-off Julie to bail me out.

A couple hours in, my cellmate arrived. He was roid rage incarnate, all flushed face and tree trunk neck. The cop escorting the man spoke to him like he would a wasted friend.

"I know, I know," he said. "Wife gets a little mouthy and things happen, but you gotta sleep here tonight while she comes to her senses."

"Like that'll fuckin' happen," the man said with a bitter laugh.

The cop grinned and unlocked the man's cuffs. "We can only hope, right?"

When the cell door locked and the cop disappeared, I watched my cellmate out of the corner of my eye. The man's knuckles were torn up. With his thumb, he rubbed blood in mindless circles. I wondered how many times he'd beat his wife and how often he'd spent the night—always just one night—in this same cell. The longer he rubbed the blood, the more his expression softened, as if the act were soothing.

I realized this was it: a chance to test my theory that The Licker was an angel sorting saints from sinners. This man seemed leaps and bounds scummier than me. If The Licker had tasted him, I had to know how he'd reacted.

Mustering my courage, I asked, "The Licker ever get you?" But the question came out small and squeaky, like a literal prison rat.

The man narrowed his eyes, seemingly both perplexed and entertained.

"Course he did," he said. "Weird first question to ask though, don't you think?"

"Yeah, sure, but how did he react? When he licked you, I mean."

The man's laugh had a mean edge to it, like he was two questions away from dunking my head in the toilet.

"How the fuck do you think he reacted? He went 'mmmmmmm' like the disgusting homo he is. You two would get along."

My heart sank. I couldn't be worse than this guy. No way in Hell. Unless I'd done terrible things in my sleep. I'd heard of it happening before. Sleepwalkers committing murders and arsons and—

No, that was insane. I knew myself better than that. I'd told white lies, neglected the dishes, and driven over the speed limit, but anything worse than that—even in my sleep—was way out of character.

So why did The Licker find me so grotesque? If I kept the question inside, it would spiral out of control. I had to let it out.

"The Licker," I said. My cellmate glared at me, annoyed I was still talking. "After he tasted me, he gagged and spat. I still can't figure out why."

The man closed his eyes, then pinched the bridge of his nose.

"I can't tell if you think you're funny or you're just fuckin' nuts," he said. "But I'm too tired for this shit."

With that, he slipped into bed and turned toward the concrete wall.

I stayed awake, wondering what it all meant. Maybe it meant nothing at all—The Licker's gag just a gag, a cosmic joke. If he slipped through these bars, licked me again, and went "mmmmmmmm" this time, would that mean something? Maybe not. Maybe the "mmmmmmmm" was a gag of its own.

But I couldn't accept meaninglessness and abandon my search just because answers eluded me. I'd have to try harder, dig deeper, sacrifice more.

The Licker could torment me all he liked, but eventually—a day or a decade from now—I'd uncover the truth.

⊗

Julie broke up with me not long after my night in jail. She seemed sympathetic when I finally confessed to my experience with The Licker, but her patience strained as my obsession grew.

I stopped coming to bed with her and started wandering the streets each night, hunting for The Licker until dawn. To a stranger peeking out their window, I might have looked like an insane and desperate man, searching for his lost dog: "Here, Licker, Licker! Where are you?"

One morning, I curled up on the couch after an unsuccessful and exhausting hunt. Julie stomped into the living room and shoved her phone in my face, brightness turned up all the way. I blinked away the sleepy blur to see a text from Julie's mom: *Are you okay, sweetie? I saw Alan walking through our neighborhood last night, screaming something. He seemed drunk.*

"Why are you doing this?" Julie asked. "Like, I get that you want answers, but this is so fucking embarrassing. Can't you just come to bed with me tonight? Like a normal boyfriend?"

She stared me down with wide, judging eyes. I didn't say anything; I couldn't lie anymore.

But my silence was answer enough.

⊗

One October morning about six months later, The Licker paid me another visit.

I'd given up my hunt for the night, a migraine inflating my skull like a balloon about to pop. I wouldn't be able to sleep without painkillers, so I bought some at a gas station. The clerk raised an eyebrow like I was some sort of tweaker—just another asshole with the wrong idea about me—but he still gave me the restroom key when I asked for it.

I entered the restroom and locked the door behind me. Inside, it was blindingly fluorescent and smelled like old piss masked with artificial lemon cleaner. Wanting to save myself from more pain, I turned out the light. In the dark, I stumbled toward the sink and opened the bottle of pills.

Just as I turned on the water, I sensed The Licker behind me—a looming presence that hadn't been there when I'd entered. A sliver of light spilled under the door, providing just enough illumination to create a dark reflection in the mirror. The most I could make out was a spindly silhouette with a head brushing the ceiling tiles.

My migraine vanished—or at least my awareness of it did—and my heart jumped into palpitations. This was my chance. I wanted to turn toward The Licker—confront him face to unknowable face—but I knew if I did, he would disappear through the door or the musty ventilation grate or the toilet, escaping in that impossible, lightning-fast way so many spoke of.

I steadied myself with a deep breath, keeping my eyes on the shadow in the mirror.

"Are you finally going to tell me why?" I asked in a shaky whisper.

The Licker didn't react. He just stood there, staring.

"Because this has been really hard on me," I continued. "I need to know what's wrong with—"

An appendage extended toward me. At first, I thought it was his too-large tongue until I made out its dim shape in my peripherals. Dangling from a limp wrist was a hand with long, thin fingers. I wondered if he wanted me to shake it—sealing some sort of demonic pact for forbidden knowledge—but he held it in front of my mouth.

I knew what I had to do. What *he* wanted me to do. But I had no idea what might happen if I went through with it.

With no time for second guessing, I closed my eyes and licked him.

He tasted like the calloused hands of a carpenter.

Like the blood of a soldier dying in battle.

Like the furry chest of a Neanderthal. The soiled ass of an ape.

Like the gory teeth of a megalodon and the clumpy feathers of a tyrannosaurus.

Like the too-salty sponges of the Cambrian seas.

Like the stromatolites springing to life before all others.

He tasted like everyone and everything wrong. A gustatory historian of this place from time primordial to the present.

And somewhere in those layers of time was my flavor, stewing among all the others he hadn't enjoyed. There were others! I didn't know why The Licker found all of us so disgusting, but I felt relieved that I wasn't the only one. He'd held onto these grotesque memories going back billions of years, unable to part with them. Not a single "yummmmm" had stuck with him.

In that way, we were the same.

The Caretaker

Katrina Monroe

Katrina Monroe is the author of They Drown Our Daughters, Graveyard of Lost Children, *and* Through the Midnight Door. *A private investigator by day, she lives in Minneapolis with her wife, kids, and Eddie, the ghost who haunts their bedroom closets.*

ᜣᜤ

Hush! Listen—

Are you listening?

It's the crows. They always have a go this time a' year, all claws and creaks and claws. Smart birds, crows. They never forget a face and, if they like you, bring you presents. They can even mimic sounds. Once, when I was a kid, I heard some screamin' in the night and near gave my daddy a heart attack with all my cryin' and carryin' on. But it was just the crows mimicking.

I—yes. Sorry. I'm looking for the caretaker, to say hello and maybe talk about an addition to the west gardens. I was told I could find him out here. The kitchen sent scones.

Yer lookin' at 'er. I can tell by the look on yer face you weren't expectin' someone like me. I'd shake yer hand, 'cept

I been diggin' in this here dirt for a bit and I wouldn't want to muss your pretty dress. Am I right in assumin' you're the new—er, that you're Mrs. Everly? I'm afraid I'm not in a fit state for such a nice lookin' scone, but I'll keep it wrapped up for later. Thank you. Too kind, too kind.

No, no. It's okay. No need to apologize. I'm used to it. See, my daddy was Everly Manor's caretaker for as long as I can remember. Up 'til he died, a' course, but that was a long time ago. Mrs. Ludlow up at the house says I'm the spittin' image, but that's just 'cause she didn't know my mother. Nobody did, but I got pictures provin' she's real. Was real. She died, too. They're buried together, Mom and Daddy, behind the hill. Loyalty buys you lots a' things, but it don't buy you a plot on the estate. That's for Everlys only.

Speakin' a' the devil, it was Mrs. Ludlow what sent you this way, right? She's a busy-body that one. Means well most of the time, and I ain't usually one for speakin' ill of acquaintances, but you'd be smart to keep one eye aimed in her direction. Don't get me wrong. She's not *untrustworthy*. She's not *unloyal*. Matter a' fact, I challenge you to find someone more dedicated to their position than Mrs. Ludlow. And my daddy, a' course.

She didn't always carry the matron's keys, though she'd be the first to tell you she deserved it more than her predecessors. Started in the kitchen—most girls who come to Everly start in the kitchen—but she had *airs*, as my daddy liked to say. Saw herself as the lady of the house, if you can believe it. But Sir—Mr. Everly—has a type. Mrs. Ludlow ain't it.

Am I Mr. Everly's type? My mother didn't think so, even when he came calling.

Oh, I wouldn't presume to know. Just the caretaker, me. I'm not one for scandal or stickin' my nose where it don't belong. My place is here, out among the flowers and the dirt and the loam and the crows. You can hear them, can't you?

Can't imagine what's got them so riled. My daddy used to say they're… whatchu call it? Empathetic. Somethin's not right, they feel it in their teeny, little bones. They'll let you know it, too.

Anyhoo, you got that ring on your finger. I'd say a question of type is, as Mrs. Ludlow likes to say, moot. And, boy, don't that ruby shine.

Mrs. Ludlow says it's an heirloom. In the library there's a whole line of portraits—women—and they're all wearing this ring. My husband's mother and grandmother and so on, I presume.

I… 'spect she's right.

I don't know much about my husband's family. No one seems to. Does that strike you as odd?

Mrs. Everly, ma'am, do you mind if I work while we talk? It's just my daddy always said idle hands do the devil's work and I'm not one for tempting trouble. These bulbs ain't gonna plant themselves, after all. Should have got them in yesterday, but I got behind with the weedin' and all after that rough rain we had this week. Made a right mess of the loose soil.

Tulips, in case yer curious. Lillies are more traditional, but Mrs. Everly – the last, er, *other* Mrs. Everly—loved tulips.

These'll be red ones, come next spring. They'll grow big and strong, cause this plot's the best on the property. Enough shade in the summer to keep cool, but enough sun to keep the grass and flowers bright as candy. There's a perfect view of it from Mr. Everly's office, or so I been told. Never been in there myself, see. It's out of bounds. Not that it makes much difference, a' course. The house is Mrs. Ludlow's responsibility. And yours now, I 'spect.

Those women—they are his family, are they not? I'm not so naïve to think he wasn't married before—the gray in his beard so deep it's nearly blue—but it was only the once, am I right? And she wore this ring?

It's a beauty, for sure. I ain't never owned anything like that m'self. I don't covet it or anything, covetin's a sin, but I'm not ashamed to say I find it pleasin' to look at it. When I was little, all I wanted was pretty things. Sometimes, when the kitchen girls snuck me in for a taste of the first batch of grapefruit marmalade, I'd wait 'til they was twitterin' amongst themselves and dip through the door, up the stairs to the house proper.

And I don't have to tell you what a beaut' it was. Ceilings high as mountains, wood fixtures so deep and polished it'll make yer mouth water. The first coupl'a times was about explorin'. Touched everything I could, like touchin' it made it real. Not knowin' no better, I licked the wallpaper in the library, thinkin' the bright, plump apples would come alive on my tongue.

Didn't take too long for my daddy to catch me, though. He weren't mad, he said, just disappointed, which hurt worse than if he'd raised the ceiling with his shoutin'. But instead of draggin' me down by my ear, he took my hand and led me upstairs to a hallway so dark it hurt to look at. *How many doors you see?* he asked me. I counted four, but my daddy had a thing for riddles, so I just shrugged, figuring—rightly—that it wasn't about how many there were. He wanted me to see 'em, to fix 'em in my mind like I would a spider with a bite that was more than just fangs.

You're talking about the second-floor hallway? Just outside the library? There are five rooms on that floor. Before he left on business, Mr. Everly instructed me not to enter the fifth, the one hidden behind a ghastly tapestry. Have you heard of such a thing? The woman of the house forbidden to enter a room in her own home?

There's them crows again, getting all antsy.

They're hungry, is all. All this upturned soil hides more than you'd think. Like I said, though, crows is smart. They'll wait 'til I leave and dig their beaks in, root around until they find something they like. The desperate ones'll swallow their finds whole. The *hungry* ones. But there's a couple that'll bide their time. Wait 'til the others have had their fill, then brush their feet through all slick-like until they find the right sort-a meal. Did you know pill bugs are like wine? The patient ones'll find a real pretty one and bring it back to its nest where it'll sit for days—weeks, sometimes—until it's just the right flavor. That's when they eat. You ever seen a crow shudder?

Anyhoo, we stood there for a long time, me and my daddy. He put out his hands and turned them over so I could see the callouses, the dirt in the creases, the stark lines of red under his nails. Don't matter how hard I scrub, he said, hands'll stay dirty. He said mine would be the same, that a caretaker's hands are strong and capable, but they're stained. S'why I couldn't in good conscience take that lovely scone from you. A caretaker's hands shouldn't touch somethin' that beautiful, not unless there's a good reason.

S'why I'm not welcome in the house, 'cept on special occasions. Weddings, and the like.

I don't remember seeing you.

Oh, you wouldn't have, miss. *Ma'am.* Caretakers aren't invited to the ceremony.

Erm—not wishin' to be rude or nothin' but you've probably got better things to do than sit out here talkin' to me. I heard Mrs. Ludlow mention somethin' 'bout family comin' to visit? Fancy that. I bet you have a nice, big family. Lots a' siblings and cousins and aunts and unc— No? But there's yer brother a'course, right? Big, strong bloke always lookin' out for his sister's honor? Who would gallop into the mouth of a dragon to save—

Only child, you say? I see. Pity. Er—not that yer parents wouldn't be pleased as punch with a daughter like you. My daddy always said he'd take one a' me over a hundred brothers.

Maybe I will take that scone now, if ye don't mind. Somethin's upset my stomach, but this'll put 'er to rights. Thank you. Lovely. Better with some a' that grapefruit marmalade I was tellin' you about, but I'm not one to complain. Some coffee and we'd have a proper picnic here, eh?

Though it'll be nicer in the spring. With the tulips.

It's my understanding a caretaker cares for the house. Sounds like you're more of a groundskeeper.

My daddy always said a caretaker does exactly what the name says—he takes care, be it the house, the grounds. A good caretaker is willin' to step in where she's needed. Most times, just happens I'm most needed out here. I'm sure you know the Everly estate is the biggest in the county, and Sir is particular about the landscapin'. He's private, see, so everything serves a purpose apart from beauty. Even the tulips here.

Private. Like with the fifth room? You've had to have seen it. Mrs. Ludlow may play stupid, but you and I are friends now, wouldn't you agree?

I don't—

And you don't strike me as stupid.

I appreciate—

So, as a friend, tell me…What is in the fifth room?

Kind of you to call me a friend, ma'am. A caretaker's work can get lonesome, all that time spent wanderin' the grounds with not but a trowel and the call a' the crows for company. Like I said, I'm not one fer complainin' and all, but sometimes it's nice havin' another livin' soul to talk to. My daddy always said you can tell a good caretaker by the content of his conversation, be it on his own or with company.

There's two things I inherited from my daddy, one of 'em bein' his gift of gab. The second is his hands. See? They're smaller than his was and not quite as roughed up, but you can see the hard spots, the dirt. The stains. "Out, damned spot," he used to say, and then laughed that sad laugh I ain't never quite understood, but always reminded me of the crows.

Another thing my daddy always said was that life is full a' lines. There's ley lines and property lines and lines in yer face and hands… and then there's lines you can't quite see 'til yer up against 'em. 'Til it's almost too late to stop yerself from crossin'.

Oh? And what's your daddy got to say about withholding information from the woman of the house? What's he got to say about duty?

Quite a bit, ma'am. Quite a bit. But if you'll beg my pardon, ma'am, these tulips ain't gonna plant themselves and if the crows is to be believed, the frost is comin' quick-like. I don't think it's too much to say that spring won't come to Everly if I don't get my hands dirty. But you enjoy your day and maybe one day we'll have a proper picnic out here, under the moss, with the loam and the crows.

❧

There, Ms. Chloe. That'll do you nice. A whole bed a' tulips. That'll prove a fine sleep. Nicer'n any bed up at the house, I'd wager. You just keep that in mind when the frost sets in and your bones tremble with the cold. Spring'll be here before you know it. I'll even bring my lunches out sometimes. Would you like that? Keep you comp'ny on the dark days.

And don't you pay no mind to the whispers. Oh, I can hear them, too. I feel 'em buzzin' through the dirt like breath through blades of grass. Siobhan can be a mean ol' thing, but she don't mean it personal. She always was the jealous type. And Katherine's brayin'll stop once she moves past the mud and into the soft gray at the other side. She lost her eyes at the end, see, and she went into the ground blind and lost. Maybe you can help her. One day. When yer ready. 'Cause, in the end, all you got is each other. All the Mrs. Everlys.

And me, a' course.

Like my daddy always said, *'til death do you part* may have been good enough for Sir, but a caretaker's job isn't done once the heart stops beating.

Now I'm not one fer complainin', but I *did* tell you all, like I told her. I did say the crows was smart. The crows'll tell you with every flap and scratch and scowl. They'll tell you about the room and the blood and the screams, if only you'd listen.

Poor girls. Ya'll never listen.

Clipped Wings

Emma E. Murray

Emma E. Murray writes horror and dark speculative fiction. Her novelette, When the Devil, *and debut novel,* Crushing Snails, *are available now. Her debut collection,* The Drowning Machine and Other Obsessions, *will be out in February 2025 from Undertaker Books, and her second novel,* Shoot Me in the Face on a Beautiful Day, *will be out August 2025 from Apocalypse Party. With degrees and a background in both psychology and elementary education, she now spends her time either writing or playing pretend with her daughter. She is represented by Clara Chuiton of Olswanger Literary Agency.*

⋅⋅⋅

I could never forget when I first saw her, red curls like wild tendrils of flame against the sea of an oversized canvas that danced with turquoise and cerulean. I'd heard her name in the art circles, seen photos of her work, and had fully expected to fall in love with a piece, probably several. I didn't expect to fall in love with her.

Cambria.

Her name matched the primordial sexual energy that oozed from her every pore and perfumed each breath. Honey-hued skin that tasted as sweet as it looked complemented dark eyes. Her curls would shimmer brightly crimson in the sunlight, then soften into muted auburn in the dark where we cocooned ourselves with comforters and tumbled together like animals. I named her "Redbird" between our pillow forts and heavy sighs. She'd titter like a bird song when she laughed, especially when embarrassed.

"Did you know some people believe cardinals are sent as signs from loved ones in the afterlife?" I asked in bed one night while my fingers traced her clavicle, my lips nibbling on an earlobe.

"Hmm?" She was always only half-listening.

"I saw you burning red against *Tumultuous Sea* and knew you were my cardinal, sent by Aadhya from the other side."

Her eyes fluttered open.

"But she drowned, Lexi. That's so morbid." She sat up and looked at the wall of color that I'd bought the night we met. "Honestly, that makes me feel kind of sick."

"I'm sorry. I just meant," I paused to kiss the nape of her neck, "she would want me to be happy. And you make me so deliriously happy. You're my little cardinal. Here, let me show you how happy you make me."

She closed her eyes as my mouth moved down her body.

Cambria exemplified pure feral beauty, and at first, I was proud of our contrast in public. The looks we'd get, my expertly pressed, full-beat makeup, pristine presentation the antithesis of her bare face and dirty hiking boots. So natural it was obscene. With her smile in full bloom, she could instantly captivate any room. Nothing pretentious or fake about her. She hardly fit into the art world, yet they couldn't help but welcome her. The supreme talent in her work was irrefutable. Naturally flawless, just like Cambria.

But time tarnished the splendor, little by little. She was always in her studio, painting by herself, or so she claimed. I had my doubts, though she'd never admit to anything, and I could procure no evidence to the contrary. Just when my suspicions would reach a fever-pitch, after weeks of supposed chambered solitude and nothing to show for it, she'd call me over, hurry me up the stairs by both hands, and reveal another oversized masterpiece.

Once there was a giant canvas of vivid red against a void of black, with speckles of glass worked into the layers of oil. She said, with a sheepish grin, it was inspired by us. Every painting was brilliant; how could I argue with her methods? Still, I couldn't stand the little hints of infidelity.

Didn't answer my texts all night?

She was caught up in painting, her phone conveniently on silent.

A too-small bra hanging in the shower?

She'd explain it away as a mindless online shopping mistake.

"Why didn't you return it then?" I'd press her, my jaw tight, but she'd shrug.

"I don't know. It was cheap anyway."

I went to shows and galleries, often alone. I didn't really mind; we could keep our work lives separate, but sometimes her absence ate away at me. Even though I loved her wild spirit, my heart often ached for the predictable comfort and early nights in, like I'd had with Aadhya.

But there was something inexplicable about Cambria that kept me coming back.

We fell into a pattern of fight, flight, and fawn: an argument ending with her abrupt disappearance, an avalanche of texts and calls from pathetic, drunken me until she finally returned, followed by my waiting on her hand and foot until things steadied out, the next storm already on the horizon. It was exhausting, and at our anniversary dinner, watching her pick at a shrimp cocktail, I realized I couldn't take it for much longer.

At least, not the way we were.

It started with the soap. It was such a little thing, much easier than I would've ever imagined. I'd expected it to weigh on my conscience, but it didn't. I hardly thought about it, even when the poison took effect. After a few days, nausea washed over her in waves, then debilitating headaches and a rash. I hated to see her uncomfortable, but it had the desired effect. She stayed home.

I heard her on the phone, canceling party plans and dinners. *Just a little under the weather. Probably working too much. Maybe you're right. Need to take some time off.*

It was music to my ears.

She'd crawl into bed and beg me to join her, just to cuddle up and watch movies late into the night, sleeping restlessly, feverish against my skin. But when the rash got worse, she decided it was some sort of dermatitis and systematically threw out everything, switching to hypoallergenic, fragrance-free versions. She started to recover, waking each morning a little closer to her old bubbly personality, but I couldn't help myself. Her illness had become like an addiction.

A dash of thallium in her eggs, carefully folded to hide any clumps. A pinch of arsenic in her nightcap, matched with the perfect recipe where a slight bitterness would be welcome and never suspicious. A drop of sweet antifreeze in her coffee. It was only the tiniest bit here and there, but it added up, and with so many symptoms, I felt confident a correct diagnosis would be unreachable.

She was often bedridden, but when she felt up to painting, she always invited me along, in case she became too weak or disorientated to make it down the stairs by herself. I played the doting girlfriend, especially when her hair started falling out in clumps in the shower and her skin turned a waxy, jaundiced yellow-green. She'd look in the mirror and cry, but I'd be there to reassure her.

Yes, you're still beautiful.

Yes, I still love you.

Yes. Yes. Yes.

As the faithful and loving partner, and having the luxury of material means, of course I called doctors who make house calls for my darling. I handpicked only the most bumbling, money-grubbing quacks to look over my love. They'd examine her, cluck their tongues, and end up prescribing z-packs, Oscillococcinum, and tinctures of essential oils.

She clung to me more than ever, but as her health spiraled, so did her untamed nature. I cut back on my concoctions, but the dark edges of depression creeped quietly inward and soon there was a heavy veil between us. Sometimes I could hardly reach her. Then came the morning of the sores, and I knew I'd gone too far.

As she'd pulled herself weakly to the edge of the bed, I'd noticed a red-tinged stain across her pillow. I figured it was from another late-night nosebleed. The faucet sputtered and then a gasp that nearly stopped my heart. Even before the shriek, I could feel some terrible truth sizzling electric through the air.

I ran to the bathroom, as she sank to the floor, curling into herself with deep, braying sobs. I begged her to tell me what was wrong, and fear gripped me as I watched Cambria's horrified, wild eyes.

"Look. Just look!"

She pulled back her lips. Red pustules erupted across every inch of her mouth, but worse were the plethora of holes, as if eaten away by acid, etched so deeply into her gumline that the ends of her teeth poked through like the gnarled, jagged roots.

Her diet was reduced to lukewarm liquids through a straw to avoid nerve pain, and a complicated routine of salves, cleansers, and wound packing took up a massive amount of the day. But I didn't let her feel alone. I was there with her every step of the route to recovery. I also switched out her toothpaste with an untainted one, for even I had become averse to the smell of decay that drifted from her open mouth as she struggled to breathe each night.

Still, I loved her. Sure, her figure had suffered, the weight falling off so quickly that she had become skeletal where she'd once been soft, but I still held her through the night. Her hair had thinned, but my Redbird still shone like copper on her pillow in the morning light.

After five days of weakness so intense she couldn't leave the bedroom, Cambria begged me to take her to the studio. She said it'd been too long since she'd painted. I had to carry her up the stairs to the studio and helped with the key, Cambria's slight weight leaning against me. The room was dark and musty from disuse. For the first time, my face flushed hot and burning bile crept up my throat.

"Are you okay, Lexi? You're so pale."

Jarred, I looked to Cambria, a silent plea in my eyes that I didn't have time to hide.

"God, what is it? You look like you've seen a ghost." Genuine concern seeped through her words, but even as sick as she was, she quickly reverted to a playful attitude. "I know it looks bad in here, but I promise I'll get it cleaned up when I can."

"Oh, it's nothing. I was just surprised at how stale the air is. Do you think it'll be okay for your lungs? I don't want that cough to get worse."

I could feel myself overacting and tried to dial it back a bit.

"Can you get that canvas in the corner? I need to start right away, before I get too tired."

I retrieved the easel and her palette, though she wouldn't let me touch the paints. Only she could mix them. I loved that she was still that same artist at heart. So, I watched from across the room as she sketched a few lines, carefully mixed some dark colors, and then dove into her process.

It surprised me how quickly her vision revealed itself, but this one wasn't like any of the other surreal visions in vibrant tones. Realistic yet distorted hands and faces in grey and tan tore at each other, wailing mouths and distended muscles stretched in pain, weeping sores and baleful eyes stared blindly. The nightmare grew with rapid strokes and suffocating speed. I found myself holding my breath and had to force open my lungs to take in gulps of air. Cambria didn't notice. Her muse had possessed her, unable to tear herself away for hours until she collapsed in exhaustion.

I ran to her and pulled her head to rest in my lap, but being so close to the abomination on the canvas made me nervous.

"I'm sorry. I don't know what happened. I think we should go home now. I've finished anyway." She was breathless when she spoke, eyes averted from her own creation.

"Why this?" I gestured toward the abyssal canvas. "This isn't anything like your usual work. Is it because you've been so ill?"

"I don't know. I couldn't stop myself." She turned to me with haunted eyes. "I paint what I see at night, and I don't see beautiful things anymore. Only this."

Once we were home, Cambria cried in the shower for three hours. She didn't eat or speak for two days. I had already begun to cut back on my concoctions, but after seeing her like this, I only used them sparingly and with extreme caution. Just a few headaches, a little nausea. But it didn't matter. I couldn't coax out even a hint of my Redbird anymore, so I immersed myself in my work.

When she found out about the gallery opening, a careless mistake leaving my mail in the open, she pried for details.

"You're going?"

"I think I'll stop by, just to check it out."

"Who is she? I've never heard of her."

"Fresh out of school. It's funny, I've actually heard a lot of people comparing her work to yours," I said with a smirk; however, she didn't react how I'd expected. She beamed, radiating genuine joy like I hadn't seen in months.

"Really?"

By her tone, I could tell she wasn't threatened, but flattered. I swallowed hard, thinking how she'd feel differently if she saw the same pictures of the artist I'd seen.

"Yeah. Maybe I'll pick something out. Do you think that'd cheer you up a bit?"

"Go for it." She turned away; she'd already faded back into the shadow of herself.

We had dinner before I headed out, and I felt strangely disgusted by our contrasting looks. Me, decked with rubies in a black satin dress, and her, in dirty sweatpants and a stained tank, bags under her eyes and dry lips. Even her wild hair was tied back and hidden under a beanie. She hardly looked like the Cambria I fell in love with. We ate in silence except for the muffled crunching between teeth.

The moment I walked into the gallery, I could better see why everyone was comparing this newcomer to Cambria. The canvases glowed with the same intensity that Cambria's had. I was immediately drawn to a cobalt blue painting, an abstract face in rapture. I leaned closer to read the title. *Blue Rhapsody.*

The song immediately flooded my mind.

"Do you like that one?" a voice asked from over my shoulder. I turned to see a stunning woman with black hair down her back and skin a deep velvet.

"Yes. Quite striking. I'd consider buying it, if the artist will let me."

"She certainly will. I'm Salome." She extended her hand.

"Salome? I would've expected you to be a dancer, not a painter."

She smiled devilishly, as if she hadn't heard it a thousand times.

"Maybe, if you stick around, I'll pull out my seven veils." She winked and my heart jumped. "I didn't catch your name…"

"Sorry, how rude of me. Lexi Bowers." I held out my hand and she took it in hers, gently, like it was something precious, not like a handshake at all. I felt myself melting.

"Nice to meet you, Lexi. I'm glad you're enjoying the show. If you're serious about purchasing anything, come find me."

Then she was gone, moving into the throng of people. I followed her the whole night, trying to keep my distance, but she was magnetic. There was a brisk rush in my veins like I hadn't felt in years. I ended up not only buying the painting I'd had my eye on but also a large piece she talked me into after showing a couple snapshots on her phone, though that was still in progress.

At home, Cambria was thankfully asleep. I was sure she'd notice the energy I couldn't help but radiate. As I crawled into bed, nuzzling against her, I hoped some sleep would be enough to get back to normal. When I awoke the next morning, I knew it wasn't. I'd dreamed of Salome the entire night, dancing with her veils to "Rhapsody in Blue."

Cambria was up before me, for the first time in months, and had somehow made her way down the hall to the kitchen. She even made a pot of coffee before needing to rest. As I entered the room, ready to make breakfast, I saw she was staring at the painting I'd brought home from the show.

"Lexi, this is incredible!"

When she turned to face me, I winced at the look painted across her face. It was a mixture of awe and worry.

"Who's the artist again? I don't feel like I've seen anything like this before."

"Her name's Salome Smithson, and I actually thought…" I paused and looked down, "…that it looked a lot like your stuff."

I could sense her face turn away, back to the canvas, searching for the similarities. I knew she saw it. All throughout breakfast, her eyes would wander back to it, linger for a moment on a detail. By dinner, she couldn't tear her eyes away from it. She just sat at the kitchen bar, staring at the canvas propped against the wall.

"You know, it makes me happy. I like knowing someone is creating things like this. The kind of things that used to live in my head…" But she trailed off, not wanting to finish.

I knew my chipper attitude was only making it worse, but I couldn't help it. Salome was all I thought of. Cambria did manage the strength for one of our old passionate fights once she found out about the other painting. It ended with us making love like we hadn't in ages, though I had to fight to keep Salome out of my mind while Cambria's tongue and touch were on my body.

But it was still my Redbird I thought of at the climax.

As soon as she was asleep, Salome returned to haunt me. I snuck out of the room, my phone lighting up the hallway.

How long until the painting is done?

A wave of guilt hit me the second I pressed send. Three dots appeared immediately. I stifled a cough as her response popped up.

It's ready when it's ready ;)

I fought through the bubble of nausea as I clumsily initiated a flirtation. Before I knew it, it was two, and I forced myself to say good night. She said she needed to go paint anyway. Apparently, her inspiration only struck at night. Cambria was always a morning person, getting up before the sun to soak up the newness of the day and mix her paints. Again, I felt sick. There was nothing beyond some innocent flirting, and yet I knew I couldn't ever let Cambria see our conversation.

I snuck back into the room and wrapped my arms around her, but her bony form felt awkward in my embrace. I dreamt of Salome, and Aadhya, and beautiful women I'd never known. Anyone but Cambria.

The next morning, I couldn't help myself. I texted Salome right away.

Can I come by later to see your progress on the painting?

She didn't respond for a few hours, but when she did, it was a yes. We sorted out that I'd come by after lunch.

The blender whirred in front of me, and I poured in the ground up pills, knowing the strawberry-banana mix would disguise it as always. Cambria swiveled on the stool and kept her eyes on the painting, chin centered in her palm.

"You need to drink the whole thing. It's got protein plus your vitamins."

I watched her gulp and grimace, the pink curtains of milkshake sliding down the side of the glass.

"It's really bitter. Did you add something new to it? Maybe too much protein powder?"

I bit the inside of my lip. Instinctively, I wiped my sweating palms against my jeans and turned away towards the sink, rinsing the blender as an excuse to hide my face.

"Oh, I guess maybe I did. Sorry."

"You're dressed up. Are you going somewhere?"

"Yeah. Need to check some stuff at the gallery downtown. Won't take long." The lie tasted metallic on my tongue. Cambria nodded, her eyes back on the painting.

I heard her mutter to herself, "It really is remarkable, isn't it?"

Salome's apartment was in the swanky part of downtown but small, dark, and smelled faintly of mildew. The furniture seemed second-hand, mysterious dark stains on a few of the cushions, and designer shoes were tossed against the wall near the front door.

It was only a studio, so I could see everything as soon as I entered, including the work-in-progress near the glass door to the balcony, outside a tangle of twinkle lights and a folding chair near an ashtray. It was everything I'd expected for the young artist, probably living from sale to sale. Cambria had been like that when I first met her, though she only spent her money on travel, never possessions. Even poised and proper Aadhya had a few habits from her youth that I had to break.

"There it is." Salome gestured to the easel. "Almost done, as you can see." I cracked a smile with a side glance, and she giggled. "Seriously, what's the big hurry? I've never known anyone who couldn't wait for a painting." As she leaned back on the arm of the sofa, I wondered if she knew the seductive nature of her pose.

"Well, it's just…" I turned away. "It's crazy. We don't really know each other at all, and yet, there's something about your art. It reminds me of Cambria."

"You mean Cambria Allred? I've heard that before. I love her stuff," she said with a half-smile that quickly wilted. "What's wrong? I don't understand."

"Cambria…she's my partner. I love her an unimaginable amount. I'd move the fucking heaven and earth for her, but there are some things a person just can't control." The tears began to flow, hot, salty, and surprisingly real, as if what I was about to say was true. "I need someone to talk to. Someone not in our circles, who doesn't know her well. You see, Cambria…she has an illness…it's terminal."

A sob rushed out of me, and I crumpled to the floor. Salome knelt beside me, enveloping me in her arms, her dark hair obscuring my vision like a shield from the outside world. She whispered, but I only made out a few cliché platitudes. "An inspiration, one of the greats" and "I had no idea" and "Yes, let it out."

Slowly, I regained my composure, but we stayed huddled together on the filthy carpet. She fetched tissues, and when I could finally look at her again, there was something changed in her face. As if something inside of her had broken, aging her slightly as it swept her into a new phase of life. My heart swung like a pendulum in my chest. I wanted that phase to be *me*.

"How long?" Her eyes were wide, unsure whether the question was allowed.

"They're not sure."

"What can I do?"

"Your paintings make me so happy." The tears threatened to rise again, but I pushed them down. "They remind me of her when she was healthy. Can I just watch you paint a while?"

"Of course. Whenever you'd like," she answered, barely more than a whisper, as I leaned closer. Her breath was hot on my lips, and I realized it wasn't my imagination, but she was moving closer as well.

In unison, we closed our eyes and the kiss happened, though I made sure to pull away and look ashamed enough to match my story.

"I'm sorry. I just—" she started, but I stopped her, my fingers against her full lips.

"It's okay. More than okay. You know, Cambria has always wanted me to be happy, just as I've wanted nothing but happiness for her. Please. Be my friend." I took her hands, clutched them in mine. "Let me watch you paint. Let me buy your work. Let me dazzle the world with your talent to keep my mind off the tragedy unfolding at home. And someday, maybe, things between us will…change."

She nodded, eyes wet as she pulled her lips inside her mouth to a tight, sad smile. The sleek hair slipped from behind her ear and fell softly across her face, and I admired its darkness, nearly iridescent in the sun shining through the window, an oil slick rainbow hiding in the depths. Salome. My magpie. My raven.

I think I'll name you Blackbird.

Protista

Jendia Gammon

Jendia Gammon is a Nebula and BSFA Awards finalist author of fantasy, science fiction, and horror novels and short stories. She has also previously written as J. Dianne Dotson. Jendia was longlisted for the Lodestar Award and two British Fantasy Awards. She is CEO of Roaring Spring Productions, LLC *and Editor-in-Chief of its publishing imprint,* Stars and Sabers Publishing. *Jendia is also a science writer and artist. Born in Southern Appalachia, Jendia lives in Los Angeles with her family.*

ᘓᗷᘔᗝᘓ

The kelp encircled the top of the great morro as a diadem of green and gold and bronze, which just before sunset caught the dying rays and glowed like gems. In that way, the morro resembled the head of a giant poking up from the sea, and so it looked that evening, before the sun dipped in the rare, cloudless horizon and sent forth one final, green spark before darkness. Wyn, or Anwyn as her birth name decreed, felt a thrill of satisfaction at the green spark. Upon that stretch of coast usually the sea intermingled with the air, smudging the horizon in a grey wash of marine layer. The clang of buoys and the low moan of foghorns became the only evidence of anything plying the waters offshore. The harbor would be smooth on those evenings, as if compressed by fog. Not so this evening, where little shuddering waves had ruined the perfect reflection opportunity of the morro upon the harbor. Wyn heard disappointed sighs from photographers at that, until the flash.

The morro provided some semblance of shelter for the harborside part of town, which sloped down from a higher hill, from which one could see the other morros, stretching eastward into land. Only this one emerged from the sea. Wyn imagined them all as gods, buried and sleeping, waiting for a time to return. But they would not that evening.

She shoved her hands into her hoodie's pockets, nudging the beach pebbles with the toes of her tennis shoes, and she listened to the soft chatter of tourists on the boardwalk along the harbor.

"They're usually out there," she heard one disappointed tour guide. "I mean, always. But not this evening. Maybe their food is harder to catch tonight for some reason."

"I wanted to see the otters, Daddy!" wailed a small child, and she heard the father's apologetic consoling.

"Let's go get some taffy and then we'll come back again tomorrow!" he offered.

Wyn heard a snatch of the children wailing, "…the *ooooooot-terrrrrs!*" and the sniffles and snorts of the small thunderstorm of disappointment. She sympathized, and then she blinked.

No otters in the harbor? The harbor was famous for that. That was odd, indeed.

The darkness seeped from the quavering stars above and poured down to the horizon, indigo paint upon both land and sea. But not the crown of kelp upon the morro. Strange-ly enough, it still glowed, as it had just prior to sunset. She looked up at it.

The tourists piled into golden-windowed restaurants, and Wyn could hear the clatter of dishes, silverware, and the bustle and hum of patrons. It was the last night of summer, and everyone had descended upon the little bayside town one final time. School would open on Tuesday, sending overly excited children away from their families and into the pensive halls of learning, while caregivers would exhale or tense up or both, accordingly.

Wyn missed those days: she often got the urge to buy notebooks and new pens at this time of the year, even though for her, school was over. She had applied to a two-year course up the coast in the north, thinking a master's degree might at least give her some sort of benefit over working seasonal jobs during high tourist season where she stayed now. She had been house-sitting for her uncle, who would return within a few weeks from a sabbatical overseas. It didn't give her much money, but it gave her an anchor, and she wondered what she would do next.

She glanced again at the top of the morro.

It shimmered.

Does anyone else see that? she wondered. Then she reasoned, *It could be the lights of the businesses along the harbor reflecting on the kelp.*

But as she tried to look at it, it seemed to fade, until she turned her head.

No: it *was* glowing. It was subtle, like starlight only seen from the corner of your eyes. But she could see some hint of the glowing even staring at it full-on.

Phosphorescent kelp? No…I've never seen it do that before. Is this a seasonal thing?

She didn't know her kelp as well as she knew the seashore animals, and she regretted it. What did she know about kelp? It wasn't a plant; she did know that. It behaved much like a plant, but it was actually of Kingdom Protista. A many-celled protist that grew like a plant, and swayed in tall kelp forests just off-shore, feeding and sheltering a vast ecosystem. It bobbed with its floaters upon the surface. She shivered. Kelp was weird.

Clumps of it would sometimes wash ashore during high tide. She often joked and called it "beach salad." But just now, the tide was out, and yet she didn't see any glowing clumps of anything. Come to think of it, she then wondered, why was there even kelp on top of the morro? Yet that was exactly what it was. She felt sure of it.

"There's no way kelp would make it that high up," she muttered aloud, glancing up at the great sea rock. "You'd need a tsunami or something."

The thought chilled her. There hadn't been a tsunami on that shore in living memory, she knew. There hadn't been any major earthquakes in several years, either. So that didn't make sense.

Could an animal have taken it up there? But that's a whole lot of kelp for an animal to carry; the only thing that can really make it up there is birds. Oh, and people. Nobody would take that up there, though, would they? Nobody's that stupid, are they?

And yet she knew that they *might* be, particularly tourists. And most especially younger ones, although that wasn't always the case. It was a slippery thing, the Rock, and she remembered that she'd seen people scaling it from time to time. But never at night. So if someone had indeed carried a big mass of kelp up there, they'd have done so during the day.

Then she saw movement on the top of the morrow.

"Oh crap, please don't be so stupid," she muttered. "If someone's up there in this darkness, with it being that slippery…"

Blinking, she rubbed her eyes and strained to see what it might have been.

She heard a shriek, and then a crunching-splattering sound.

A scream rang out across the harbor.

"Oh God," she whispered, and she ran toward the boardwalk.

Her legs burned as she bounded over the shoreline, trying her best to avoid twisting her ankle on some of the larger pebbles, and she nearly tripped over the remnants of an old beach fire, its long-chilled logs catching her shoes. Still, she kept running.

She skidded to a halt on the dockside part of the harbor, her feet thumping upon the old, grey wood. She looked this away and that for anyone's reaction. But no one was around.

The diners in the restaurants hadn't noticed the scream, she realized. In fact, no one else seemed to. Only her.

She swiveled up and down the boardwalk, panting, and shoved her chin-length brown hair down into her hoodie. All the shops were now closed, and she realized they were closed for the season; the only people left alongside the harbor were the diners, as the town wound down. Summer was over. And by the sound of it, so was someone's life.

Not finding any open shops to enter and ask for help, she rushed into the closest restaurant, "Whale Now Fish n' Chips." Its warmth and light greeted her, and for a few seconds she gasped with relief, coupled with her exhaustion. She held her side from the stabbing pain of a side stitch. The hostess looked blithely unconcerned as Wyn doubled over, gasping.

"Someone's hurt," she wheezed. "Someone's out there," and she attempted to point behind her, triggering the pain of the side stich again. She grimaced. "I think…I think they fell. Like from the Rock."

The hostess calmly cleaned the laminated menus, and never made eye contact with Wyn.

"Do you hear me? Someone's hurt!" cried Wyn, yet the young woman continued rubbing the menus.

A grey-haired couple walked past her and said, "Good night! We'll be back next year!"

The girl beamed at them and chirped, "We'll miss you! Thank you!"

The couple walked within inches of Wyn, ignoring her completely.

She stared them down with pleading eyes, squeezing her hands together.

"Help!" she cried. "Someone fell out there! Someone's hurt!"

Yet they walked by her, uncaring, and left the restaurant. Wyn was appalled.

"Can anybody please help!" And by this time she'd shouted it.

No one budged.

She blinked, horrified, and backed out of the restaurant. The door shut. And all the lights within vanished.

She stared. It had gone silent as well. She rushed forward again and pulled on the door handle; she found it wet. And it was locked. She pressed her face upon the windows and could see nothing inside. No light, nothing. Complete darkness.

She could hear something, though, so she jerked around.

She slapped her hand over her mouth. The harbor churned and swirled and formed a great vortex within it, like a drain, sucking down. Broken buoys and nets and crumbled boats whirled around in the darkness—for now there was no light anywhere.

Except for on top of the morro.

And there she beheld it: slinking down, drifting, twisting, snaking: the glowing kelp, growing like hair upon the head of the great sea rock. It shot down like so many cables, and it shot toward *her.*

Her breath caught in her throat and the turned to run, away from the shore, up the hill. But a whipping sound sang through the air, and she felt a barbed tug that yanked her ankles, and she fell upon her face.

It was upon her: glowing green-gold, thorned kelp, its floats wheezing like lungs, twisting around her, pulling her in. The rush and roar of the great vortex of the harbor hid her screams.

But no one was around to hear them anyway.

She was being pulled up.

Up.

Up to the top of the morro.

It had her, it entangled her, it stung.

And then it released her upon the crown and snapped all around her in many strands as she sat in immense pain, weeping. She gazed out at the landscape, and no light shone anywhere, up and down the coast; she could see for miles. The sky was clear, full of cold starlight. The only other light came from the ferocious kelp.

It swayed all around her as if under the sea in its own forest, tall stalks shooting up from the sea floor, higher than the highest trees, all bending and twisting around her.

She had no way down.

Then she heard a savage roar, like a jet engine, and she jerked her head to gaze west.

Something was coming.

A great undulation.

Tsunami? She thought desperately, terrified. The land would be inundated, crushed, and she would be…

"Safe," a deep and quiet voice told her.

She looked all around, as the glowing kelp lashed and whipped in a phosphorescent dance. She could see no one.

"No," she whispered, and then upon the seaside the great wave thundered and foamed, and she clutched herself and trembled. The kelp surrounded her, as if she were a baby bird in a glowing nest. She covered her head and wailed. The town warped and snapped as the water surged.

And then with a long, sinister hiss, the water retreated.

Then, silence.

Shaking, she opened her eyes. The forest of kelp had retreated too, but some strands still surrounded her. Looking down, she beheld a ruined coast, stripped of all buildings and trees, complete devastation in the darkness.

Sobbing, she wondered how she would ever get down, and if anyone were still alive.

"Safe," the cold, soft voice said again.

"Let me down! Please!" she begged. "I need to go…home."

"You are home."

My Dog's Ghost Story

Breanna Bright

Breanna Bright has a master's degree in English and is the author of In the End *and* The Shepherd and the Horned Girl.

CRED

My dog and I have a ghost story to tell you.

I know your first question, so I'll get that out of the way: She's a medium-sized mutt of indistinguishable origin, the color of coal. My friend called me very late one night, having discovered the stray in her car (no, we don't know how she got inside the car) and said, "We've got a situation here."

So, her name is Situation.

When I first met her, she looked at me with eyes I felt akin to. She had the same expression I have when I look at myself in the mirror in the morning.

Please help me. Please be kind.

Someone had clearly not been kind to Situation. I took her

in for my friend. We spent the next three days hiding in the bathroom, eating food that was bad for us. I called in sick to work so that I could give her medicine and fill the air with encouraging words that she couldn't understand. She latched onto my tone though, tapping her tail shyly against the linoleum.

I said more nice things to her in those three days than I've said to myself in years.

Here's the thing about Situation: She is haunted.

The haunt started to manifest after we left the bathroom. First was the smell. I noticed a scent around her, like lit matches that had been blown out. I gave her several baths, but it didn't go away.

I took her for a walk one morning, then came home and brushed my teeth. When I came into the kitchen, she was on top of the cabinets, in the gap between them and the ceiling. About eight feet off the ground. She was shaking with her tail between her legs. I almost broke my back trying to get her down.

Another time I took her on a walk in the park where a small boy asked to pet her. Situation gratefully received the attention, but then, as he was scratching her ear, she said, "You will die in the spring of your fifty-second birthday, child."

He cried and ran away.

"What the hell was that?" I demanded. "You can talk? See the future? Or was that bullshit? But you can *talk*?"

Situation just wagged her tail gently. Her eyes begged me not to hurt her. When we got home, I tried again.

"I heard you talk, why are you hiding it now? What's your deal?" I bribed her with sandwich meat; she got very confused and excited, but didn't talk.

That's when I started to get suspicious. It didn't seem like my dog could talk. She didn't behave like someone who could talk. (I considered that maybe she was just a really good actor, but then caught her dragging her ass over the carpet, and felt that no one who could talk would go that far.) I began making theories, and watching her closely.

I didn't have to watch that closely. One day, when I got home from work, I found her floating in the air, ears brushing the living room ceiling. Her tail was tucked, and she looked at me, her expression begging for help.

Situation wasn't doing this on purpose, and *she* wasn't talking. Something else was.

I managed to pull her down by her front paws, and she stopped levitating once they touched the floor. She huddled up against me fearfully, not leaving my side for the rest of the night.

At work the next day, I searched 'can dogs be haunted?' on my phone.

It made sense to me. When things float and you hear voices, it's generally agreed that the place you are occupying is haunted. But this wasn't a place. It was a dog.

The world wide web wasn't very helpful in that aspect. Some people claimed to see ghosts following their dogs around, assuming it was the original owner who had passed away. Nothing about them floating or delivering dark omens.

"Reading ghost stories?" Tania had glanced over my shoulder at my phone as she walked by. She carried a box of new DVDs that were tagged and ready to go on the shelf. I slipped my phone away and helped her. Various angles of women's naked bodies looked back at me as I put them in the appropriate categories.

One would think our store would have gone the way of other movie rental places, but people like the anonymity of renting physical copies of porn. No search history, and if you pay cash, no evidence at all.

I had been here long enough that I had my own sorting system for the videos. Girl on girl was what I called the 'Carpet and Scissors' section, guy on girl was usually in the 'Vanilla Crème Pie' section. For nurses, teachers, and construction guys you needed 'Occupational Hazards'. Then there was 'all tits', 'all ass', 'all dick'…there were many ways to sort porn and alphabetically wasn't the most efficient. If someone came in asking for step-sibling stuff, that was the 'Keeping it in the Family' section. If someone just wanted to watch masturbation, that was the 'One is the Boneliest Number' section.

Boredom tends to lead to puns.

"You like spooky stuff?" I asked, adding a video to the Girls Gone Wild shelf. Tania was what is referred to as a 'work bestie' (not the friend who found Situation in her car). I preferred her over the others that worked in our erotic film store, and not much work got done when we got to gabbing.

"Oh yeah, Jason, Michael, Ghostface, I'd fuck 'em all," Tania said, pausing to squint at a title called 'Jesus Christ Serial Rapist.' I wasn't sure if that went under 'Religious' or 'The Weird Stuff.'

"Which Ghostface?"

"Mickey's the hottest, but I'm not picky."

"Are there any movies where a dog is like…possessed?"

"Uh, maybe? Cujo isn't possessed, he has rabies." Tania gave up and put the film on the 'Staff Recommendations' shelf.

"No, I'm talking supernatural. How do you get rid of ghosts in movies?"

"If they don't swallow the house at the end there's usually an exorcism of some kind—circle of salt, burn sage, yell as the ghost throws you across the room."

"So, you know a lot about this stuff? Ghosts and the super-natural?"

"I mean, just what I've seen in pop culture, I don't know any of that witchcraft stuff."

"I mean…you know more than me."

The jingle bells hanging from the store's door ding-a-linged as someone came in, hurrying past us with their eyes on the floor. Looked like they were making a bee-line for the 'Rear Window' section.

"Hey, Tania?"

"Yeah?"

"You want to see something weird?"

⬥

She was off work two days later and came over late afternoon, coerced by the promise of pizza. I had been worried that Situation would be completely normal for Tania's visit, and if that was the case, I would have sent her to a kennel and myself to inpatient mental health care.

But Situation was not secretive, or rather, the ghost wasn't. That morning she had brought me a dead dove, which in itself wouldn't be unusual behavior for a dog except that its head had been removed, and dead man's fingers grew from its neck.

"That's great, Sitch." I sighed and left the bird on the patio to show Tania.

Flies had also started to follow Situation, buzzing all round her like she was dead—even though it was the middle of winter. She sighed at me sadly as they went for the corners of her eyes, and I killed them off with bug spray.

When Tania arrived, I invited her into the elderly duplex I called home. 'Duplex' was inaccurate though. The building had once been a regular house, but the landlord had managed to split it up into three apartments, including the basement.

All the construction was DIY'ed, and something was always breaking or not working right. Currently, the thing not working was the heating. I kept the space warm with a single space heater that I moved from room to room as I migrated through the house—bedroom in the morning while I got dressed, bathroom for showering, and living room for everything else.

I had worried about leaving Situation alone in the house. I couldn't afford to get a crate, so I returned the first time expecting to come home to chewed walls, puddles of pee, and eviscerated electric cords. But Situation had proven herself to be very obedient and well-mannered. For the most part she just wanted to sleep on the pile of old fleece blankets I made for her. A good walk and a good meal was all she really asked for.

Situation rose from her makeshift bed as I introduced Tania. They acquainted themselves splendidly. Tania loved animals, and Situation loved to be loved. I didn't have to tell Tania to keep touching the dog, she rubbed on her for several minutes. Then Situation looked at her and said, "It wasn't an accident, your dad threw himself off that cliff."

Tania screamed and ran away.

Dogs don't have mouths like a human's. While Situation was speaking English, her elongated snout struggled to form the words. Her long tongue twisting and her loose lips going taut. What came out wasn't a cute speech impediment like Scooby Doo, but a mangled, snarling mess of the spoken word. It dropped a cold stone of horror into my stomach every time I heard it.

I looked at Situation. "The levitation thing would have been better."

When I stepped out to check the mail I found that Tania hadn't actually left. She was sitting in her car, looking at her phone. When I tapped on the window she rolled it down.

"You don't have to stay. I was just hoping to get some advice."

"I almost left, but I have a friend—she does witchcraft, reads palms and shit. I've been texting her. I told her what the dog said, told her you had no way of knowing about my dad. I don't tell anybody that he fell off a cliff when we were hiking. Was she telling the truth?"

"I have no idea. I've written down things she's said to other people, but there's no way to prove them. At least, not for a while."

"Show me what else she's said." Tania pushed out of the car, stomping back to the door with an air of anger that she was no doubt trying to get to replace her fear.

When we came in, Situation came up to Tania and wagged her tail excitedly (new friend!). Tania flinched.

"I don't think it's actually the dog," I explained, grabbing my notebook. "It's not Situation saying these things. I think the dog herself is haunted."

Tania frowned as I showed her the page of Situation's past messages. Each included a description of the person she spoke to:

Small boy (6? 7?) "You will die in the spring of your fifty-something birthday."

Woman, young, jogging—"Your womb is barren. All your children will miscarry."

Biker dude (thought I was a ventriloquist, was not amused. We ran away.) "Your mother knew what your stepdad was doing. She did nothing."

"Holy shit," Tania shivered. I pointed out another page. This was a list of all of Situation's supernatural occurrences along with the date and times they happened.

"This isn't just ghost shit, this is like *The Exorcist*—demons and shit."

I stiffened. "She's never hurt anyone."

"I think I should stay over for a few days and observe her. I'll also bring my friend in to get her opinion. Is this all Situation has said? Does she give *you* omens?"

"No, actually. I can pet her all day long but she's never spoken directly to me." I proved it by rubbing Situation's stomach until she was mush with her tongue hanging out in bliss.

"Strange, because you're her owner? But you said it's not really Situation doing these things."

"If Situation could control her levitation all the treats on top of the fridge would be gone."

"Okay. Let's take her on a walk."

We observed Situation all day, with Tania taking vigorous notes. She told me about what she had seen in movies—how the behavior seemed to line up with a possession.

"But a dog is an odd choice for a demon to possess," she admitted. "Like, we can *kill* a dog."

I gave her a horrified look.

"I don't mean that we'll have to!" she backpedaled. "But, with a dog, if an exorcism doesn't work, we *can* just put it down. Not like a human."

"Do you think we should exorcise her?" I asked. Situation glanced over her shoulder, as if making sure we were still there, giving us a big, tongue-flopping smile.

"I have no idea. Let's wait until Niagra gets here, and then we can try some things. Hey, bud, you want to pet our puppy?"

A little girl was having a walk with her dad who was pushing a stroller; she couldn't have been more than three. I glared at Tania, but the toddler was already running up to Situation and putting her arms around her neck. Situation licked her cheek in return.

I willed the little girl to go back to her dad, but he was taking his time walking up, and the child was perfectly happy giving Situation all of her attention.

"Okay, that's probably good—"

"Your choices on March 22, 2059 will result in the deaths of three people," Situation said in that horrible, dog-mangled speech.

The little girl stared at her, then started to laugh so hard she fell over and farted.

"Daddy, the puppy talk!" She managed to gasp out before laughing again. Dad picked her up, gave us a silent nod, and went on his way.

"Tania, I don't want her doing that to kids."

"I'm sorry, I needed to see it for myself, but you're right, that was wrong. At least the kid thought it was funny. She probably won't even remember."

We went back to my duplex. I ordered some pizza and we ended up just kind of watching Situation. I played ball with her, showed off the few tricks she could do, and gave her claws a trim while Tania observed.

"You're right. She doesn't try to hurt you, or anybody. She seems like a perfectly normal dog."

"That can talk and fly."

"I mean other than that. When did this all start?" Tania asked, clicking her pen.

"A few days after I got her, about a week ago." I told her the story about how my friend had found Situation in her locked car, having no idea how she got in.

"Did you ever post her to a lost dog board? Check for a microchip?"

I couldn't stop myself from dropping my face into my hand.

"I'm so stupid."

"Dude, you haven't taken her to a vet?"

"I was going to!" I defended myself. "I was waiting for her to calm down first, you know? She was already so scared. Then the haunting shit happened and it totally left my mind."

"Do you think we could take her to a vet without incident?"

"One way to find out."

⚘

Situation was chipped.

The vet was having trouble finding the registration in their system, however. They said it was old, and it might take a bit to track down the last owner. While we were there they gave her a checkup, and I watched nervously, waiting for her to do something weird, but the appointment passed uneventfully. I was handed a bill that I had no way of paying.

When Tania and I returned to my house, a car was parked in the street out front. Tania perked up excitedly, declaring that her friend Niagra had arrived.

Niagra was a tall Hispanic girl with amazingly artistic nails. She squealed in greeting when Tania gave her a hug.

"Girl, I know you hitting me up with that spooky shit, I'm 'bout to start my own business. Get in on them rich haunted homes, know what I'm saying?"

"I hear ya, girl," Tania nodded, "but this isn't a haunted house. Let's go inside."

"Hi, I'm LaKrisha," I introduced myself. "This is Situation."

"Y'all named your dog Situation? I love it, girl. I got this cat from my sister, he's a black-and-white so my nephew named him Oreo. Kids are so cliché, you know? I wanted to name him Catsby, you know, like Great Gatsby? Leo was rockin' that tuxedo."

"Love that movie," Tania agreed.

Inside, I made glasses of tea for everyone.

"Y'all still working at Ghetto Porn?" Niagra asked (That wasn't its real name. The building was unlabeled so all the locals called it Ghetto Porn. If it has a real, official name, I don't know it). "My cousin got his photo on your wall of shame that time he stole those edible panties. He was wondering if you could lift the ban."

Situation pressed her nose into Niagra's crotch. Niagra scooted away, but Tania encouraged her to pet the dog.

"Go on, give her some loving."

"Don't break my nails, pretty girl," Niagra cooed. "Aw, you're just a baby, aren't you? You're just a big 'ol—"

"Your real name is Carmen Isabella Ren Veste," Situation warbled.

"Nuh uh."

Niagra was up and out of the house.

Tania and I chased after her. I was still holding two glasses of tea, condensation soaking my hands. Tania called for her friend, and Niagra turned, a look of relief suddenly washing over her face.

"Oh em ghee, this is a prank show, isn't it? Like the fucking Stranger Things kid! Oh my god, that was so good, holy shit, you scared the hell out of me."

I looked down at my feet. Tania sighed.

"It's not a prank show. This is why we called you over. Situation is haunted or possessed or something. We need your help."

My hands were cold. I turned back to go into the house, letting Tania talk to Niagra about the situation with Situation. I was tired, due back at work tomorrow, and feeling overwhelmed by everything. I wanted my dog to be okay, but if I just kept people from petting her and pulled her off the ceiling now and then, that wouldn't be so bad. I needed three more days in the bathroom.

Tania and Niagra came back inside. The ice had melted in their cups but I passed them over anyway and dried my hands. Niagra read through my notebook, catching up on mine and Tania's notes. When she was done she set it aside and stood up.

"No time like the present. Let's just start doing stuff and see what works."

First, I poured a circle of salt around Situation, then pushed Situation back into the circle and swept the salt back into place. Niagra lit candles. Situation's wagging tail scattered the salt. I swept it back. Niagra requested sage but I didn't have any, so she wrapped some bay leaves and expired basil from my pantry in parchment paper and burned that, circling Situation with smoke. The dog lowered her head fearfully at the smell of fire, whining pitifully.

My heart ached. "You're scaring her…"

Tania took my hand and squeezed it. We sat on our knees outside the circle. "It's okay, it's just for a second."

Niagra spoke rapidly in Spanish. Mine wasn't fluent, but I picked up enough words to determine that she was telling whatever was possessing the dog to get out.

As Niagra raised her voice and chanted her command, Situation began to respond. First her eyes rolled back, showing only the whites, then she started to rise into the air.

"Mierda."

Tania grabbed my arm. I couldn't take my eyes off the dog. Her tail went between her legs and her mouth opened, contorting to try and make human words.

"When trumpets sound and seals are broken, war will rule and souls will be a token by which angels and demons trade…"

The scream of my fire alarm interrupted the ritual. Niagra yelped in surprise and Situation fell back to the ground. I went to her, kicking salt away. She scrambled, slipping on the hardwood floor as she tried to get traction. She dodged my arms and ran down the hall.

Back into the bathroom.

I sighed.

"What was that? A prophecy?" Tania gasped. Niagra was panicking, running her bundle of herbs to the sink. I grabbed a chair and boosted myself to the ceiling to reset the alarm. When silence returned, we all stood in the smoke and salt. I smelled something off and looked down. Situation had pissed on the floor.

"I'll get it," Tania said, pushing herself up on shaky legs. "You check on the dog."

"Paper towels in the kitchen," I said, stepping off the chair.

I found Situation curled up between the toilet and the bathtub, her big eyes shining.

Please help me. Please be kind.

"It's okay, baby." I closed the door and sat down, holding my arms out. "No more, I promise. You can be weird all you want, I won't hurt you."

Slowly, Situation came out of her hiding spot, tail tapping hopefully against the porcelain. I wrapped her up and hugged her tight, scratching all her favorite spots until she conceded to the love and began licking my cheeks.

"Good baby, my sweet girl, you're okay. We won't do anything else." I sighed deeply and leaned back, taking her face in my hands. "I just want you to be okay."

Tap, tap, tap, went the tail.

CR&O

"So, what now?" Tania asked. The three of us were on the couch with leftover pizza. Situation was still in the bathroom. Niagra shrugged.

"I don't want to scare her anymore," I said. "It doesn't matter if she floats a little. I just won't let strangers pet her and it'll be fine."

"What if it's not? What if it gets worse?"

"I'll cross that bridge if I get to it. She's a *good dog*, she's not evil or anything. Just…kind of weird."

"Kind of," Niagra rolled her eyes.

"But don't you want to know why?" Tania demanded.

"Of course, but not at Situation's expense."

My cell phone rang. I glanced at the screen and saw it was the veterinarian's number. Heart leaping, I quickly answered. Niagra and Tania leaned in when they heard my voice pitch, trying to hear what was going on.

I hung up the phone.

"They found the owner."

Their spines went rod-iron straight.

"Who is it?"

"They said the entry was glitched and some information was lost, including the name, but they managed to contact him—some guy named Bree. Guess she was lost last week."

We all exchanged eye contact, waiting for the others to ask one of the many questions swirling through all our minds.

"Does this guy *know*…?"

"Did the haunting just start?"

"When are you meeting him?"

"Guys." I held up my hands. "I know that Situation is scary. She flies, she talks, she's given some pretty freaking premonitions. I should be rushing to get her back to where she came from, but…when she came to me, she was scared to death.

She didn't leave the bathroom for three days, and…I get that. I know it's stupid to relate to a dog, but I think she was hurt, and I've been hurt too, and I'm not just sending her back to that. Not without knowing she's safe."

"Even with the talking flying thing?" Niagra raised a manicured eyebrow.

"Even with that."

Tania sighed. "Alright, well, guess we better come with you then."

"You don't have to."

"Oh, we're going," Niagra cut in. "This I've *got* to see."

⟰⟱

Bree was a white man in a suit and hat, leaning against a black sports car outside of Taco Bell. The neon sign painted him a startling purple and red. The veterinarian had helped delegate a meeting spot where I could return the dog that very evening. But when I drove up beside Situation's owner, only Tania and Niagra were in the car with me.

The three of us stepped out. I gave Bree a careful wave. Niagra stayed behind me, but Tania took the lead, eager to get to Situation's backstory.

Bree narrowed his eyes at us, no doubt suspicious at the lack of dog.

"Hi, I'm LaKrisha. I know we were supposed to bring Sit—um, your dog, but I had some concerns that I needed to talk to you about."

The man opened his mouth but Tania jumped in. "Do you know she's weird?"

Bree snapped his mouth shut. I heard his teeth clack together. "You've had her for a week?" He asked.

I nodded.

"It's surprising that you're alive." He glanced away, staring at something in the distance while his phrase hung in the air. "I'm aware of the canine's idiosyncrasies, what I don't know is why she is not here considering what you've no doubt witnessed."

"Well, that's what I was trying to say," I said around the lump in my throat. "When I found her she was really skittish and scared, she didn't like to be touched, and, well, I don't want to make baseless accusations, but she showed signs of… abuse."

His eyes slowly turned from their far-off gaze to look at me and I felt goosebumps cascade down my back.

"We're in the middle of training," he said flatly, challenge in his expression.

"I hope you'll understand, but I can't return her unless I know she's going to a safe home."

Bree took a step forward. Tania's hand clamped down on my arm and I felt Niagra shift forward to stand at my side.

"Hey, yo, that dog got rights," Niagra said, holding her hand out to keep the man from stepping closer, "and my girl got finder's rights. We can take you to court if we suspect abuse. I looked it up on the Humane Society's website."

"Let me get this straight," Bree said, crossing his arms. "You have witnessed the animal's strange behavior, but you insist on keeping her because you…are worried about abuse?"

"She's a good dog," I insisted.

"When you say 'strange behavior,'" Tania leaned forward, "are we on the same page? You know about the floating, right? The talking?"

Bree turned his unsettling gaze on Tania and she shrank back. "Her eyes see the evil in men's hearts, she shits brimstone, and will be a companion to demons at the end of days."

That explained why the Wal-Mart bags I used to pick up her

poop always melted.

The three of us were stunned into silence until I said, "…the other day she got scared of a piece of lettuce."

A sharp snap of the eyes back to me, a moment of tense silence. Tania's hand was still locked on my arm. Then, Bree smirked. The smirk turned into a smile, and the smile into a laugh.

It was the most awful sound I'd ever heard. This time all three of us shrank away, shoulders rising defensively.

Finally, he stopped laughing, even wiping a tear away, and turned back to his car.

"You know how to reach me," was all he said before getting into his vehicle. I stared, mouth literally dropping open as he drove away.

"That's it?" Niagra watched him leave the Taco Bell parking lot. "Is he going to fight us on this?"

"I don't know," I said, watching the vehicle disappear down the road. "It didn't seem like it."

"Holy shit. Guys, he knows what Situation is, he said he was training her…" Tania whispered. "He was talking about brimstone and shit, like she's a hellhound or something."

"My dad told me a story about Perro Negro—Black Dog. An incarnation of the devil." Niagra crossed herself.

"She's a good dog," was all I said in answer. "Come on."

The three of us got back in the car, and I stopped at the pet store on the way, grabbing some toys and treats now that I knew Situation would be staying long term. Back at the house the other girls returned to their cars.

"See you tomorrow, I guess?" Tania asked.

"I'm in at five," I confirmed. "We gotta clean up the 'Unreasonable Standards' section."

"That one the anime?"

I nodded. Tania smiled. "Keep notes for me."

Back in the house, back to the bathroom, I introduced Situation to her new toys, which she seemed very pleased with. Some tug-of-war with a rope allowed me to get a closer look at her eyes.

They always seemed brown, but there was a hint of red in there.

The two of us played until she felt brave enough to come out again. Together we hit the couch and put on a movie. Situation snuggled close.

"Good girl."

Symboyotic

Adam Fall

Adam Fall is the manager of Underbrush Books, in Rogers, Arkansas and hosts their monthly book club. He is currently working on a collection of relationship-based horror stories.

CREO

The ceiling never looked so barren. Blank. Its texture like Jackson Pollock designed a monochromatic painting for the blind.

Ilana stares, fixated on the parallel wasteland above her. The steady thump of the headboard tapping in a steady 4/4 beat. No deviation. Consistency. A drummer's rhythm.

He's a nice guy, she thinks. Maybe *too* nice, if not only a semi-capable lover. They had texted an appropriate amount of days before meeting up at the bar downstairs for drinks. Subtle perks of living above a bar: never having to risk going to their place. People get murdered that way, or so she heard.

Three drinks. Her suggestion of going somewhere more private. He didn't miss a beat. Yes. He still isn't.

It wasn't so much that she regretted sleeping with him. After all, she came when he went down on her, which isn't a given these days. Ilana faked the second orgasm. He seemed like he needed the extra push, lest he never finish and keep pumping into her pelvic bone until it shattered. Tiredness settling into her soul.

A whimpered sigh. He rolls out from between her legs, condom drooping like a sad, wet party hat at the end of a quickly shriveling accordion of flesh. All around, the musk of sweat and pheromones blankets the room in a heavy layer of shame. A fog of emotional unavailability.

"That was…" He reaches across her unmoving form for the water on her bedside table. "Whew. Sorry. Gotta rehydrate if we're gonna go for round two." He gulps down her glass of water, winking at her and sucking in his gut.

"Oh. Uh. I've actually got work in the…"

"Seriously, babe, that was the best sex I've ever had in my life." He put some stink on the word *ever* that seemed both too serious and flippant.

Ilana forces a smile. Babe? Really? Ugh.

Their stickiness mingles somewhere between skin and sheet. An uncomfortable aftermath of a mingling of souls. Two human beings existing at polar ends of the spectrum, pressed together beneath a popcorn ceiling in the suburbs.

"I was thinking…"

When? When was he thinking? Did he internalize it in between thrusts? Or was he fingering her in the pattern of writing out a to-do list? Ilana rolls her third eye.

"…Maybe this coming weekend, I don't know, maybe we could go out again. I was thinking…"

There he goes, again. Thinking. Who told him it was up to him? Double ugh.

"…once we get another couple dates under our belt, my parents are coming to town for a weekend in late July."

Jesus. Fucking. Christ.

"They'd love you. I mean, who could help it, really." He laughs much too loud in her ear. "I just think it'd be nice to get that out of the way early. Make more time for us." Scooting closer, he nestles his matted hair against her bare shoulder.

If she could have thrown up inside the depths of her soul, Ilana would have purged the three drinks and dinner.

"Does that sound good to you?"

"I really don't know…"

"You don't have to answer now, though!" His desperation is palpable. Another layer to the fog enveloping them.

Ilana keeps her mouth closed. There's no use. He'll be much easier to let down easy with some distance. Taper off responding to his texts. Disappear back into the anonymity of the digital void.

Silence creeps into the cracks between their muffled breathing, his occasional attempts at conversation.

His pillow talk in dire straits. More like bedside manner.

The urge hits her like a fucking truck. Pee o'clock. Gotta make sure to clean things out down there afterwards or else it's UTI central. All aboard. Choo choo.

But he's finally quit. Not quite asleep, but breathing the tiny heaving breaths that come before. She decides to risk it, because more conversation is easier to grit your teeth through than a full bladder and the prospect of six more silent hours. Too tired to piss. Too full of piss to sleep.

Inching toward the edge of the mattress, Ilana attempts to unearth herself from his dead weight, break from his damp body. Hairy legs tickle her toes as she pulls away, feet finding purchase on the cold hardwood floor. Her lower half, free of the top sheet and comforter, is shocked awake by the powerful gust of the ceiling fan. Goosebumps roll like thunder across her abdomen. She's nearly free.

A mop of messy auburn hair all that's left between her and the sweet relief of an empty bladder.

Careful not to wake him, Ilana puts a hand beneath his resting head. If she lowers it slow enough, gently enough, maybe he won't notice, she plots to herself.

With the heavy mass of his thick skull supported under her right hand, she begins to slide her left shoulder across the balled up sheets toward freedom.

A tug of pressure between her shoulder and clavicle issues a panic response. She's stuck. Like his hair is made up of the tentacles of a sentient undersea creature, each strand coated in suction cups, tugging and pulling her back to bed. Using her midsection as a fulcrum, her legs the lever, Ilana digs her heels in and pushes off.

Nothing.

She is stuck, quite literally, to the right temple of her one-night stand.

Her legs kick hopelessly against the bed frame, hoping for any extra leverage. Pain explodes along her chest.

What the actual fuck, she screams into the recesses of her mind. How is he holding onto me right now?

Brushing aside his bangs reveals the answer to her question, whether she wanted it or not. They are connected. Like. Conjoined twins. Skin to skin. Flesh to flesh.

Ilana laughs. She actually laughs. She's much too drunk for this shit. Real life doesn't work like this. Real life is full of pain and awkwardness and disappointment, but in real life, people don't just *stick* together. No. Nope. Her relentless denial becomes a weapon.

"Hey. Wake up." Panic overtakes her, she shakes him. "Wake the fuck up, dude."

His eyes open wide. Instant focus and clarity takes over. "What seems to be the matter, darling?" His voice drips with sincerity and malice. "I must have dozed off." His laugh had turned sour.

"I have to pee."

"Well then why don't you get out of bed and go, silly goose." His eyes are cold and serious.

"I'm stuck. Your head…it…" Ilana couldn't quite bring herself to say it out loud.

He lifts his head up. "Was that so hard?"

"But…I tried."

"Sweetie, it's no problem. I sleep pretty soundly anyways. Go ahead and go to the bathroom. I'm not going anywhere." Again, he winks.

She scampers desperately away from the bed. Each footstep freezing against her flushed skin. Relief floods through her body as she empties herself. The alcohol leaving her brings about some modicum of sobriety. Post-pee clarity. Walking back to her bedroom, the impossibility of the situation is hilarious. She resolves herself to be single, maybe even celibate, forever.

Climbing into bed, Ilana sinks into the depression in the mattress where she had just been. To her dismay, she clambers forward beneath the sheets, subconsciously seeking his warmth. Companionship.

"Welcome back. How'd everything go?"

What kind of question even *is* that? She feels her ovaries shrinking like raisins in the sun.

"I went pee. Not much to write about there." She goes to scoot away from him, regretting the spooning already, when she feels a familiar tug.

"Where do you think you're going? I thought you wanted to cuddle." He sounded annoyed.

"I just want to go to sleep." Ilana's heart jumps within her chest. She knew she had to play it cool.

"I'm just glad this happened. You're really special. Ya know that? I'm sure girls like you hear that all the time. But it's true. Promise." His silky voice sang soft and sweet like a lullaby. "This is the beginning of the rest of our lives. I can see it now. You want kids, right? You would make an amazing mother."

Her eyes remain closed. Arms retracting back into herself, raking against his sides. Subtlety impossible at this level of closeness. Every movement she makes, noticeable. Every word he says, a micro aggression.

That tug. It's still there. Her arms can't retract any more. They lie pressed into his ribs. His back glued firmly to her breasts. Legs intertwined like vines, twisting into a sort of human braid. Her face the only piece of her with any independent movement left.

"Do you believe in perfect moments? I do. I think that, as I've gotten older, I've realized the importance of living in each and every moment. Savoring it. Committing each visual to memory. The way you look at me. How it feels to touch you. I take it all in. Drink deep from the well of love. For it is deep and never ending."

There was no doubt about it: Drunk or not, their bodies were stuck together. Ilana is transported to a land far beyond fear, further still from acceptance. She begins to flop desperately against him. With him. Her body struggling to move independent of his. Her neck strains as she keeps it from touching the space at the back of his neck.

A boyish giggle springs from his chest. "What are you doing

back there?"

"I think you should leave," she pleads shakily to the room.

Schlurrrpp pop schlurrpp

Wet and undulating, a suction forms between them. Each struggle to pull away brings her slipping closer to his back. Devouring.

"Seriously, my parents are going to be so happy for us. They ask every time I call if I'm planning on settling down soon."

Their legs are the first casualty. A new creation.

The

Crackling pops explode beneath the covers. Bones bend and break, twisting like tightly braided rope, grafting themselves to each other. Blood vessels rupture and splash the sheets in a warm, slick spray of force, only to reconstruct and meld back together again.

White hot pain rushes through Ilana's mind. She is overwhelmed by it. Consumed by it. It becomes her very sense of being. Her identity is pain.

Her pronouns are oof, ouch, my bones. Every memory of her life is wiped clean. The only thing that remains is a wasteland of hurt.

He continues his headlong descent into her.

"Can I say something? Like, really say something without judgment?" He speaks this over the muffled remaking and merging of their shin bones. Ilana's protest is masked by what sounds like a gunshot. Their Achilles tendons detonating, reconvening in the apology of a tightly bound kiss. "I think I'm in love with you. Like, actually in love. I've never been so sure of something in my entire life."

Words uttered as a backdrop to the excruciating process of rebirth. Love is the center of it all.

"I can't believe we just met. It's like I've known you my

whole life." Words echo off the white walls. The cadence of things said before, rehearsed. The pain not even registering on his face; less of an inconvenience than a fly flitting deftly across his brow. He wrinkles his brow at it. Nothing more.

Their thighs were next. A metamorphosis, a transformation, a fusion. Every new sensation of agony building and crashing against the shores of their union. Ilana's neck straining at the surface of the covers, veins rippling and tendons screaming as she desperately retreats away from the crook of his neck. Gasping for what might be her last breath, all while her knees forget how to open and close.

Once again their waists writhe and dance together; no rhythm this time. A soft and squelching pop as his penis is turned backward between their mermaid-like mess of legs, and stretched like taffy.

two

"We should get in contact with your doctor to get that IUD out. I mean, right? We're not getting any younger over here." Lips peel back in a grin. "I can't wait for our future together! I can't believe how lucky we are," he coos with the gentleness of a viper.

Ilana tries to protest. Her vocal chords, still her own, refuse to form any coherent noise. Internally, she pleads with a God she doesn't believe in. One that can't exist. Couldn't. Doesn't.

become

Her bellybutton begins to dilate. Muscles contract and relax as a hole forms in the center of her. The smell of iron permeates the bedroom. Sex and latex and freshly laundered sheets, their odor wholly consumed by the organic stench of creation. Ropes of intestine unwind from within her, like colored silks pouring forth from the sleeve of a party magician. They drip with mucus and blood and whatever other fluids exist in the deepest part of us. Unfurling, they wrap themselves around their changing bodies; slipping wetly and squirming under their stationary forms, only to wrap around again, constricting any movement from the remaining limbs.

Her breasts are no longer her own. Were they ever? She can't remember anymore. A sense of relief rushes through her. A literal weight lifted.

one

"What if I didn't leave?" He posits the question to the room, to us. "Obviously I can go back to my place and gather my stuff, but what if I didn't ever have to *leave*? I could just move in. Domesticate and enjoy our sweet little lives together. Babe?"

Pain had lost all meaning. Ilana sobs into her pillow. The muscles in her neck losing strength. It was only a matter of time now. She is afraid to disagree with his prognostication of their future; what would he do if she refused? Maybe she was already dead.

Her neck gives out, falling limp against his—theirs. In a sweeping motion, his neck twists on its axis, hers with it. An orchestra of cracks and pops play a final masterpiece, building to a stunning crescendo. With a final, body-shaking shudder, their neck completes its fifth rotation.

flesh

"Ilana, sweetie, will you marry me?"

Lips, no longer hers, move in silent protest.

"…what He has joined together, no one should separate." Matthew 19:6

Shoal King

Markus Justin Williams

Markus J. Williams is a poet, painter, and writer, who also dabbles in photography, videography, and composing. His most recent work can be found in The Encyclopocalypse of Legends and Lore **by** *Encyclopocalypse Publications, which features one short story and two poems of his. He lives in Sacramento, California, with his partner and their two cats.*

❦

Upon the banks of the foggy sea,
I let the creatures into me.
Those of whom beg to swim
Beneath the folds of my skin.

I proffer open arms and let them embrace
Me with salty kisses I've longed to taste.
Sliding through skin, and invading my veins,
These creatures and I are now one in the same.

In the pale of the moon, I wade into the water,
And begin to feed upon a passing flounder.
A man apart, but returned to the sea, I'm now whole—
Once more a part of the collective shoal.

Off the banks, in the foggy sea,
Live these creatures inside of me.
Those of whom beg to swim
Beneath the folds of your skin.

The Tales of Charles Sley

Ghost in the Gas Station Bathroom

Rebecca Cuthbert

Rebecca Cuthbert writes dark fiction and poetry. She is the author of In Memory of Exoskeletons *(Alien Buddha Press) and* Creep This Way: How to Become a Horror Writer with 24 Tips to Get You Ghouling (*Seamus & Nunzio Productions*). *A hybrid collection,* Self-Made Monsters, *was just released by Alien Buddha Press, including an introduction by Laurel Hightower. See* rebeccacuthbert.com *for publications, reviews, and more.*

 C380

I hate cleaning the men's room at the gas station where I work.

He's there every time I open the door with my mop and bucket of bleach water. Middle-aged with pitted cheeks and the look of a cornered animal—eyes wild and rolling. He's scrubbing his hands at the sink: frantic, blood everywhere. It's spattered in suds on the mirror and soaks his sleeves to the elbow. It covers his shirt—I can see it in the reflection.

And then, each time, he turns around—toward the door, and I don't think it's me he's seeing—his eyes go wide and he opens his mouth in a scream I can't hear. His body spasms; holes open in his chest. One in his forehead. And he goes down. Half a second later, and the bathroom is empty again. Just the usual piss on the walls and garbage on the floor.

The first time I saw him I had a panic attack and had to go home. I'd just started as third-shift cashier, needing extra money after my divorce. The second time I saw him I only sobbed, but my boss didn't believe me and accused me of seeing a spider instead.

I don't talk about it anymore, and I guess seeing him regularly has made him a little less scary—and being less scared, I got curious. Now, I kill the empty hours at work by thinking of what might've happened to him. I made a list on the back of a receipt:

1.   He killed someone in a fit of passion—a married lover whose husband hunted him down, chasing him here and kicking in the bathroom door before hitting him with five bullets.

2.   He killed someone in a robbery gone wrong—no one was supposed to be home. He tripped an alarm, ran, and was found at this gas station after a BOLO went out. The cops used a battering ram on the door and put five bullets in him.

3.   He was innocent. The blood all over him is from someone he tried to *save*, maybe a stranger, maybe someone he loved. And police chased him, so he ran. They found him here and shot him five times before he could say a word in his own defense.

I've tried to talk to him once or twice. Dumb stuff, like "Hello" and "What's your name" and "I'm Tina, I work here." He's never responded. I don't know if that's a choice or a condition of his penance. To go through it, again and again—*scrub scrub scrub, bang bang bang bang bang*—without being able to talk about it.

What's really fucked up about it all, though, is that I've gotten kind of attached. I still hate opening that door each night, but now, after what—five months?—if he weren't there, I think I'd be disappointed. Lonely? Because the other guy who works the shift with me—Donny—wears headphones the whole time, restocking shelves to what sounds like 80s hair-band ballads.

So, in a way, it's just me and the ghost, whoever he is. *Was.* Whatever he did. And I know I could play Nancy Drew—investigate clues, track down witnesses—but I won't. The truth is always less interesting, and every solved mystery becomes just another sad story. And the world is already too full of those.

❧

Tonight it's slow. Tuesdays always are. Not many folks out needing gas or lotto tickets or beef jerky or whatever. A couple folks in to buy six-packs. One lady needing three bags of chips. Donny left early, claimed he had a headache. I didn't care. He's not really here when he's here anyway.

But at about 2 a.m., the bell above the door rings and I look up from the doodle I'm making, and it's *him*. The guy. The ghost.

My mouth drops open. I freeze. Then I see his eyes, wide and glassy, and the knife clutched in his hand. I think, *That's a huge knife. What does he need a knife like that for?*

And I'm still wondering when he's around the counter, in my face, towering over me, and it seems like no time has passed, like he was in the doorway and I blinked and now he's not, now he's *on* me—that big knife against my throat, the other hand gripping my shoulder so hard I know it's already bruising. He's spitting at me, talking, but through his teeth, and God he smells. Body odor but something chemical, too. And burnt hair. Sweat runs down his neck into his collar. He's furious. I haven't done anything to him, but he's furious.

I manage to hit the silent alarm under the counter, and I want to put my hands up, like people do in the movies, but I can't raise my arms; my muscles have turned to water. He's blocking all the light and taking all the air. I can't breathe. He whisper-yells at me to open the cash drawer, and I do, shaking so hard it takes me three tries to hit the right buttons. He grabs the money, not that there's much, and shoves it down the front of his pants. He won't take the knife away. I think he'll go but he doesn't. He's swearing at me, "Where's-the-safe-open-the-fucking-safe-you-fucking-bitch-fuck-open-it-stupid-whore-fuck-fuck," on and on, and I know he's high as a kite, not in his right mind, but I try explaining there is no safe. We don't have a safe; we do two cash drops a day at the bank. The manager does. I tell him all this, tripping over the words and saying it again, but he isn't listening, and he grips my shoulder tighter and I cry out from the pain and he shoves me against the rack of cigarettes and they fall around our feet with soft little plops.

I don't know how I get from there, standing, to the floor, lying on my side several feet away. I cough. I cough and spit; I'm bleeding. It's coming from my mouth. I spit it on the floor. I try to feel my stomach. My hand won't move. It's underneath me. Pinned. I can move my eyes but not my neck. The man's boots step over me. The knife clatters to the tiles near my head. I'm cold. I need to turn off the air conditioning. But it's

March. There is no air conditioning. It's March. I'm so cold.

A cop comes through the door, gun drawn. There's another behind him, yelling into his radio. They run past me. I can't roll over to watch, but I know they'll find the man in the bathroom. I know he's trying to wash his hands, and I know they'll never come clean. Too much blood. All of it mine.

I know what happens next, too. I've seen it so many times.

There. The shouting. The gunshots. I count them: *One. Two. Three. Four. Five.* In the bathroom, the man is falling.

I close my eyes.

And there it is. Mystery solved, and I was right. Just another sad story, not so interesting after all.

Reeled In

Steve Neal

Steve Neal is a neurodivergent, English-born writer currently surviving the chaos of Washington D.C. with his supportive wife and less supportive cats. As an author of the delirious and strange, he enjoys poking at the unknown and seeing what comes crawling out as long as it isn't spiders. His debut novella To Love a Dying World *releases in 2025 through Off Limits Press. Follow him on Twitter @SteveNealWrites.*

❧

Ready to go?" Harrison packed up his tackle box. An older man, hunched over, moving at the meager pace his body allowed in its later years, strands of white hair falling across his brow.

"Gonna give it another hour, it can't be that dead out here." Douglas shook his rod in its makeshift stand; shoved into the netting of his chair's cup holder.

Harrison sighed and shut his tackle box. "This is holding me hostage, you know?"

"There's only so many CSI reruns to watch, Dad. Here, last one." Douglas dove his hand into the cooler to his left and handed a dripping can of Coors Light over to his father.

"I do accept bribery," he said as he took the beer and opened it with a hiss.

The pier was always theirs. A hidden piece of The Gulf no one else knew about. According to Harrison's tales, the pier went back generations, originally maintained by Douglas' great grandfather. Though now decrepit, worn down by a bitter sea and marred by split boards and barnacles, it remained a familial hideaway. A spot far enough from the known tourist beaches that no one tanned on nearby strips of sand or bobbed inside the exiguous surf. A dozen miles from ever-present fluorescent lights washing away the stars and smokestacks billowing out noxious man-made clouds. Access hidden by overgrown saw palmetto and Florida privet that reached across the boardwalk like passing lovers. Forgotten by the locals, reserved only for those of a single bloodline.

"It wasn't always like this, ya know," Harrison said after a few more minutes with a still spool.

"You've mentioned it a time or two. I'm forty-three, Dad. I remember how it used to be." Douglas did his best not to sound annoyed. These ruminations accompanied the end of every trip now, demanding a return to the good ol' days when fish bit regularly and a day trip would feed multiple households.

"Might be time to hang this up," were words that he'd never uttered before.

"What?" Douglas turned his head to the side with slack-jawed shock.

Harrison shrugged. "Listen, I ain't saying we stop these trips, but," he sighed. "Maybe this is one of those dead zones now. I read about 'em. Too much shit in the water, fish stay away. When was the last time we caught anything bigger than a pinky?" He looked out toward the horizon through squinted eyes as he spoke to the sun's final sliver.

"It's not about the fish. This is our spot," Douglas replied.

"Hell, I don't know that? But sometimes, you gotta let go what's gone."

"Maybe it's the season or—"

"Doug," Harrison's attention snapped to his son. "I don't like it as much as you do, but we should say goodbye."

The pair sat in silence, watching the last sunset they'd see from their unofficial slice of coastline. It didn't feel right to Douglas; a punishment for something they didn't have a hand in. He'd read articles about the changing waters. Either too warm or too cold, not enough salt, too much pollution, mass migration as the oceans contended with man's influence. Myriad things to blame, but not a father and son who caught less than a dozen fish a month. To leave it behind was to accept it as a casualty in a war they weren't aware they fought in.

"Shall we?" Harrison said after the last sliver of sun disappeared behind the horizon.

"I guess—" A shimmer to the ocean cut off Douglas's acceptance of the night's end. What, at first, looked like the reflection of the moon warbling with the undulation of small waves. But it moved in the way reflections couldn't. A purposeful dart to the side against the current, followed by a sinuous trail that left a silver wake, as if the moon leaked into the ocean. "What the fuck?"

The effulgence swam around beneath the surface, rapid circular movements, as if it chased something.

"That can't be a fish," Harrison muttered, getting up from his chair.

"Moves like one." Douglas pointed to the serpentining light, how often it swam back on itself, the sudden changes in direction, diving deeper, nearing the surface. Common behaviors for a predator trying to outwit its smaller, nippier prey.

"It's got that, uh, bio, like angler fish." Upright, Harrison started snapping his fingers trying to recall the proper word.

"Bio-luminescence? Yeah. That's…not normal," Douglas's head bounced around with the fish's movement.

"The Hell is it doing up in the shallows?" Harrison leant forward, peering down into the waters.

"Deep sea predators can't find food, so they hunt higher. It's a climate thing, I think."

"Maybe that's where the fish've gone. All in that thing's gut."

A second light joined the fray, quickly followed by a third and fourth, until the abyssal sea was alight with newcomers. Countless lambent silver orbs lit the sea until the inky waters turned a soft purple between the lights. Whatever the creatures were, sat underneath their natural beacons, hiding their forms. A breath-taking sight, typically reserved for neon-lit sections of aquariums housing phosphorescent jellyfish.

"Certainly one way to say goodbye," Harrison muttered.

The group continued to dart around, slowly closing in on the pier, until they surrounded the beam supports, swimming beneath and around the construction. The pair's heads shot from side to side, trying to track the school.

"It's gorgeous," Douglas said a second before the spool on his fishing rod started screaming as the line unwound at ferocious speeds.

Both he and Harrison grabbed for it before the rod flew from its makeshift holster into the surf.

"You only went and hooked one of the bastards," Harrison yelled as the pair struggled to get the rod under control.

The deep-sea interloper was frightfully strong and equally

rambunctious, twisting the line, easily fighting against the set tension. The pair dug in their heels, trying to steady the rod while providing enough slack to fight the fish without having the rod ripped from their hands. Harrison braced himself against the top of a support pillar, pushing into the shin-high log for extra leverage.

"Feather it, increase the drag," Harrison barked.

"The line'll break," Douglas grunted back, straining to anchor the rod against his forearm as it whipped around with the fish's frenzied movements.

"Can't losing this fucking rod."

On his father's orders, Douglas increased the drag of the line with his index and middle finger, testing the advertised strength of the line. The fish would tire out, stop for a moment to reorient itself and the battle would turn. It always did. The pair struggled the rod up to forty-five degrees to turn the fish's head toward them, but even with the increased tension it wasn't ready to relent, continuing its descent to the depths.

Below them, the lights moved away from the dock in unison. Curious prodding and exploration switched to an alert retreat. The school scattered, as fish were wont to do when one was hooked, but these creatures did not dissipate in every direction from widespread panic. All of them rushed toward where the line dipped below the surface, hurrying toward their wounded brethren, willing to throw their bodies and lives at whatever was brave or stupid enough to attack one of their own. Apex predators that weren't evolved to know fear. The spool whined at a pitch nearing a dog whistle, pulled in every direction. They attacked the line, ripped at as if it were the tentacle of some great squid.

"Let go," Douglas barked, noticing how little of the line remained.

"It was your grandfather's. We can tame it." His voice was strained, concentrated on maintaining his grip.

"Dad, let it go now," Douglas took his hands off the rod, reaching out to grab his father, but the line ended, exerting pressure on the pole and ripping it toward the sea. Whether by over-confidence or blunted reactions, Harrison didn't let go. A grip of steel trained by years of manual labor and marathon fishing trips ensured he followed the rod's trajectory, dragged onto the support stump before tumbling into the water.

Douglas yelled and scrambled, flapping at the air, trying to grab any part of his father to stop his descent. He crashed to his hands and knees, dangling a hand over toward the darkness below, hoping to see silver wisps of his father's hair floating around the surface before he emerged.

He scanned the sea, looking for any hint of Harrison before spotting a wake, a rapid disturbance moving away from the shore.

"Let go, you old fuck," Douglas muttered as he stood, tracking his dad's body as it moved a few inches under the waves.

The first light moved, spinning around in place before it rushed toward his father. A few others broke away from the attempted liberation of the hooked fish, racing toward Harrison's position.

Douglas didn't think at all, grabbing the knife from his lure box before diving into the water. He swam with the blade in one hand, cutting through the icy waters, nostrils and eyes assaulted by the salt. Among the tumult, Douglas could no longer track his dad's movements, nor could he see the amalgamation of lights illuminating the water. All around him was roaring nothingness. Sound warping as the waves lapped over his ears. He swam toward his dad's last known location, hoping the old man was smart enough to let go of the rod and its memories and let it disappear into the depths. No fish or sentimental rod was worth his life.

"Dad," he screamed out between strokes. "You out there?"

Only the roaring and crashing replied. An empty expanse in front of him, stretching outward infinitely, an abyss below.

"Doug," he heard inside the ocean's static. "Help."

"Keep shouting," he yelled back, desperate to audibly lock on to his father.

"They're around me," garbled words returned, shouted through mouthfuls of saltwater.

"Don't kick your feet."

As Douglas crested one of the miniature waves, he saw his father's head bobbing along with the waves, panic-stricken eyes swiveling around. He was lit from below, a silver glow illuminating his face from below as if he held a flashlight to tell stories in the dark. Only ten yards or so away, reaching him seemed possible. Hopeful.

The sound that followed was part-wail, part-gurgling. Over the waves, Douglas saw the top of Harrison's head as it dipped below the surface. Without thinking he dove into the dark, looking through squinted eyes lashed by saltwater. They weren't far. A collection of the lights moving back and forth like firing pistons. Douglas could imagine the inquisitive bites that came along with them, prodding attacks with mouths full of curved, needle-like teeth. The images of chunks pulled away from his father's body, plumes of blood drifting among the waves to attract the rest of the school to feed off the wounded animal.

Lights seared his eyes along with the salt the closer he swam to them. In the center of the movement, Douglas made out the form of his father illuminated by those surrounding him; he thrashed, attempting to swipe at the lights as they continued to nip and peck. Two more orbs came from behind, latching onto his father's shoulders and dragging him backward faster than any fish should be capable.

Douglas attempted to scream, releasing a stream of bubbles around his face, spuming on the surface as the only indication he was below. Void of breath, he stopped swimming and allowed his body to float upward. Beads of saltwater hid the tears streaming down his face when he emerged. Overwhelmed by the shock, frustrated by his body's inability to chase those evolved in the water, he could do nothing but sob as he looked out over the obsidian ocean and the few visible lights of fish lingering near the surface.

He couldn't concentrate on them. Loss clouded his eyes as much as his mind. Didn't pay attention to their movements as they closed in on him. Only when the shimmer of resplendent water danced across his shirt did he realize he was next for the starving predators.

With a kick of his feet, Douglas twisted his torso and tried to close the distance to the pier. The wooden structure seemed miles away, a hope as absurd as the idea of out-swimming those bred for hunting in water.

The first bite, a probing, curious attack, sliced into the side of his big toe. Douglas screamed out but continued to swim, desperate to feel the scrape of a rising shoreline, sand and rocks beneath his fingertips. He looked down, hoping to see anything but the bleak emptiness of the open sea. Instead, he saw a light. Its rapid ascent. The unavoidable impact. One that hit like a cannonball to his sternum. It stole his breath, forcibly extracted the air from his lungs. Douglas gagged, unable to inhale; only capable of jagged gasps that captured no oxygen inside spasming lungs. It came with no sharpness. No spilled blood or lost flesh. A purposeful, debilitating attack meant to halt retreating prey. What followed was a barrage. Countless teeth and mouths snapping at his flesh in singular attacks before darting backward to the abyss. Some took layers of flesh, others scraped at the skin, leaving surface cuts that leaked a few drops of blood into the water. The same attack he saw on his father. The rapid bites, the faster retreats, what Douglas agonizingly learned were not timid, testing bites but attempts at clamping onto him and dragging him down. He couldn't escape, breathless and floating, free for the fish to nip and pull at until one managed to extend its jaws wide enough to wrap around his ankle, thin teeth piercing into his achilles. Hooked, the fish started its swift descent, down and away from the distant shoreline. There was no time to take a breath even if he could. Precious seconds of air left before he'd start to spasm and his vision faded. Perhaps a more peaceful option, giving himself over to the ocean, drifting into weightless unconsciousness, letting go to become one with nothingness.

Revenge inspired him otherwise. With what little energy he had left, he reached down toward his ankle. Refusing to go peacefully and drift among the dark, he snatched by his feet. He expected the slimy scaliness of a fish, but this thing was rough like a piece of coral. It writhed in his hand, tearing his palms with its scales, widening the wounds in his ankle as it struggled. Douglas doubted the knife would break its natural armor but still brought his free hand down, wriggling the tip of the blade in between its scales, sawing at the creature until he felt it separate.

The descent stopped. All pressure on his ankle relented. With the severed fish still piercing his ankle, Douglas struggled to ascend, propelled by weak kicks with one foot. The lights around him retreated, only far enough for their effulgence to slightly dim and become distant, grey bulbs watching from the safety of the dark. Predators that never witnessed a death on the hunt, never encountering man's penchant for brutality.

At the surface, Douglas gasped and sputtered, bruised lungs struggling to suck in oxygen. He spun, finding the measly glow of civilization in the distance. The shore a haze of purple and shadow, the dock lost in the night. Too far to swim without the bruises and blood loss, the distance now as likely to be his downfall as the hunters.

"Can't die," he muttered to himself. "Not now."

He brought his knees up, wincing as his injured leg moved, aches pulsating out from the holes in his heel. Untold bacteria or poison surged through his bloodstream. He tucked the knife into his waistband, and reached down with both hands, grabbing the severed piece of whatever latched onto him. Douglas held what felt like the top and bottom mandible of an eel. Despite its decapitation, the creature remained obstinate, its grip held with a tension matching its brick-like texture. Each inch was a fight, emphasized by the feeling of snapping bones reverberating through Douglas's palms, as if he had to break apart the beast to remove it.

He gave a cursory glance around at the ocean. The lights seemed brighter, not as dulled by the sable sea. Perhaps closer. Impossible to tell with such a brief look. He checked over both shoulders. They encircled him. Pack hunters as desperate for flesh as they were for vengeance. The warmth spread, tingling and numbness up to his knee, reminding him of the task at hand.

Time and spilled blood would only embolden the hunters. He had to free himself. Be big, be noisy, hit the water with the decapitated remains of their kind as a warning for those brave enough to try him.

He slid the last remnants of teeth out of his heel, feeling

every barbed millimeter as it carved past raw flesh, Douglas cried out. What he intended to be a warrior's defiant roar came out as a whimper, oscillating and weak. He lifted the head above the water with both hands and smacked it into the waves multiple times.

"You're next, you horrible bastards," he screamed out at the lights. Larger. Closer.

Douglas looked at the kill in his hands, held it a foot in front of his face. It was not the expected head of a fish, nor the jaws filled with arcuate teeth dripping with sea water and venom. What he'd severed was more akin to a coral hand, three finger-like protrusions, each tipped with a syringe-like nail. What Douglas held was the end of an arm. A dead, removed limb, pallid and void of any of the luminescence he'd watched dance in the water. If it washed up on the beach, no heads would turn, no investigations or biopsies performed; another piece of loose reef washed ashore.

Around him, the lights brightened further, closing in on him in tandem. Arms of a single creature intending on attacking as a unit rather than the solitary strikes and grabs it attempted before.

Douglas pulled the knife from his waistband, circling around in the water, ready to attack whichever appendage neared him first. When he faced a group, they slowed, like children timidly creeping forward, caught red handed in their approach. It made him spin faster, knowing those behind him moved with great fervor. He couldn't protect all sides at once. The blow, a familiar, concussive attack to his lower spine numbed his legs. More followed, rapid, debilitating blows to his hips, kidneys, and shoulders. His arms fell to his sides when one struck his neck, numbing his entire body. Douglas was thankful he couldn't feel the subsequent attacks to his sternum and stomach, only the increasing pressure on his chest. He was even more thankful that the darkness seeped in from the sides of his vision, waning consciousness as they dragged him below the surface. It wouldn't hurt. In his final moments, Douglas watched as part of the seabed approached from the dark below; an oblong patch of sand rising toward him. Lit with the same argentine radiance as hundreds of lights danced around the stones and corals; thin, ashen appendages playfully coiling around themselves like eels, mimicking unsuspecting prey for curious bottom dwellers. More shot up as he approached, expediting his descent with embedded hooks in his flesh. Closer, the patch of ground cracked in its center, disturbed sediment clouded the surrounding waters, as rocks tumbled away from the opening. A perfectly camouflaged hunter, disguised as the ocean floor itself. The creature opened its maw, exposing a ribbed gullet capable of swallowing a boat whole and consumed its second meal of the night. It sank back to the depths, nestling into its hole, its mouth flush with the ocean floor, indiscernible among the innocuous sand, waiting for the next disturbance above its new home.

Flesh & Blood

Katrina Carruth

Katrina Carruth (she/her) is a newcomer to Maine, the unceded Wabanaki Homelands, where she lives with her husband, their unruly toddler, and an exceptionally grumpy cat. She's a professional chef turned horror writer with works published in Cosmic Horror Monthly and Sarah Gailey's Personal Canons Cookbook. Find her on X @katrinacarruth and Instagram @katrinacarruthauthor.

⊰⊱

Blood trickles down my thighs in a stream free enough to flow the length of my gangly legs, stopping at the thick hem of my socks. The foyer mirror rattles and I plunge the scalpel into my skin again, and my mother's eyes *not my mother's eyes* finally appear in the mirror.

It's working.

I push it in again, twisting even deeper, and her sunken, sickly face surfaces as if it were next to mine. I expect her to smile, to beam with pride at my success at manifesting more than just the same blips of her chaotic energy I managed over the last several months. Instead, she screams. I'm shocked that I can hear her cursing so clearly, livid that the trickle isn't running as freely as hers had. Always disappointed in her own blood.

Before today, I'd only ever used the scalpel on brighter days, referring to it as an X-ACTO knife while slicing colorful shapes and patterns for countless, wholesome craft projects. I never considered using it for this until I found her.

Mother's face begins to fade so I continue, this time on my arm, wincing with each slice. The look of longing in my mother's eyes *not my mother's eyes* startles me, and my grip forces a deeper cut than I'd intended.

It hits me, a little too late, that she didn't come to see *me*. She came to see *this*. I should have known.

My arm throbs, and nausea spirals up my throat as I process the sensation. I hadn't expected it to work and certainly hadn't considered the fact I'd likely need stitches if I tried too hard. I should have known I'd try too hard. I clear my throat, making sure to cough out any shakiness that might give away my anxiety. "Mom," I say as she screams. "Mom," I say louder and louder, over and over until she closes her mouth. "I think I went too deep," I manage to say.

She's silent as her eyes meet mine.

I hurry to try and fill the silence, the only way to test her ever-shifting waters. "Um…" I catch myself stuttering, then take a deep breath and continue. "…I'm bleeding pretty bad."

Her haggard gaze morphs in a split second, and the apparition of my mother *not my mother* stares at me from the mirror, her body frozen and frigid in place, fury holding her blurred form intact. "We don't need the hospital," she hisses through gritted teeth.

My mouth is dry and gritty as though it's full of sand and I stutter, failing to keep my tone calm. "No! That's not…c-c-can you just tell me—"

"We're not going to the hospital," she says again, voice booming over mine. I glance nervously from my fresh wound to my mother's *not my mother's* expression. Her eyes scour the room as if lost and desperate to regain any memory that might keep her tethered to this place.

The same ones that keep *me* tethered to this place.

I've always been the person who watched horror movies and yelled at the screen, aggressively opining what I would do in the pathetic character's situation. I'd never put up with that, never just stand there and take it, not spend another second in that house or with that person. I'd defend myself, move away, live in a box all by myself forever and ever if I had to. I'd do everything the character isn't doing.

I'd do everything I'm not doing.

Blood continues to seep delicately toward my wrist as little drops hit the floor, and I watch my mother's eyes dilate into focus, as if suddenly remembering when the rush of blood was hers. Either way, it's technically all hers; her own flesh and blood.

Her elderly mutt—the one that unfortunately outlived her—staggers around the primed-but-not-yet-painted wall, wagging its flimsy tail and temporarily distracting her. Fiery pain sears through the bits of exposed, throbbing flesh, and I drop the scalpel onto the carpet with a muted thud.

My mother *not my mother* doesn't notice. Doesn't seem to remember the events of the last five or so seconds. Perhaps I needed to go deeper after all.

The slickness gushes between my fingers as my mother *not my mother* gushes lovingly to the dog in a voice that's always and only ever been for her pets. Her arms reach out, inviting it for a warm embrace. I tell myself I don't care, but years of anguish and longing for the same invitation, same embrace, same tone to be offered to me, stirs from a place that runs deeper than my newest wound.

I tiptoe to the bathroom and crouch beneath the sink, relieved to see the first aid kit still sitting in the cupboard. The dusty one that hasn't moved since my childhood & seems to automatically replenish whatever is taken from it. I probably need stitches, but the one person I'd ask to confirm my suspicion is occupied.

My hands tremble as I press the ancient gauze against my arm, but I lose the precious hold I have on the bandage as a loud *thump* rattles the bathroom mirror.

I wish I could block her out, lock the door with a click of finality, a blatant signal of defiance—my choice to patch this up instead of running bath water.

But locking the door would never work. She's here to stay and, I guess, so am I.

She shouts about the audacity to stop what I was doing. I hear her woosh away from the bathroom, her thunderous voice rumbling like an old vacuum as it rattles the baseboards. A familiar yet triggering mom-woke-up-angry sound.

The rickety door slams back against the once beautiful mural adorning the bathroom wall—the one my mother painted when children made her happy and she dared to dream of beaches and ocean waves. Maybe if I'd been a good daughter and taken my mother to experience such things, I'd still have *that* mother. I wonder who she was when she painted the mural, and I question which mother is really my mother—the one I remember covered in paint and laughing in casual overalls, or the defeated and unpredictable one haunting this place?

I open the door as the haze of her ethereal shape returns to the doorway, and her eyes soften at the sight of the bandage haphazardly clinging to my aching arm. She glides toward me and gasps at the swollen, bright red gash. "That needs stitches," she says, lovingly. Even standing in front of me, I miss her.

"O…okay," I stutter. "I should probably go get those stitches—"

My mother's *not my mother's* eyes instantly shift back to their harsh deadness as the chill of her spirit bolts from the room, huffing and puffing to blow her world down.

I hesitantly follow her to her room, but she stops just inside the doorway, staring straight ahead into her so-clean-it-almost-smells-like-chlorine bedroom. The one I've maintained but left barely untouched.

She slowly turns around and her eyes meet mine. They're kind again, blinking innocently like a child who doesn't understand what they've done to deserve their punishment. Her lips pout as if she's tempted to throw an actual tantrum. Glancing down at the gauze in my hand. She whispers, "Go to the pantry."

I do not want to go to the pantry, but I obey. I've kept the walk-in space exactly as she left it, with homemade canned goods well past their expiration dates and bins of clean, empty jars waiting to be filled.

I return to her holding a clean jar and a quiet, tearless sob escapes her. She instructs me to place the gauze into the jar, and I do. She stares at it in my hands for a few seconds before demanding I put it away, and I know I can only imagine the complexity of thoughts racing through her mind.

Pushing aside a quart jar with the folded Barbie my mother insisted I was too old to play with and a pint jar with a perfectly preserved sandwich she tried to eat right after my father died, a space just wide enough for the jar in my hand appears.

No matter how crowded the shelves get, there's always room for another one. I twist the lid on and place it with the others, sealed tight and never out of sight.

The jars make me uncomfortable, but even I find myself addicted to the blips of life she clings to. Hospital bracelets, the infant blanket I'd once accidentally coiled around my own neck, shattered bits of her favorite China set, her mother's curlers. It was unfair the way they once taunted her as she struggled to understand why her insomnia medication wasn't working. I asked her once what would happen if she threw them away, shattered them as they crashed into the trash and were hauled away forever. She said she tried, but the jars came back. She warned me that one day I would understand, but I didn't want to believe her.

This was a mistake, bringing her back. And selfish. I should have known she'd see the jars. Should have known I was summoning her to suffer all over again. "Mom?" I ask, trying to keep my voice peppy.

She sniffles, signaling the urge to cry, and answers without looking back at me. "Yes?"

"I need to run an errand," I say, leaving it at that.

"Sure," she says without taking her eyes off the jars. "Better leave now so you can get there before it gets dark."

"Yeah," I say, letting my eyes linger on her for the last time. "Love you," I say. I mean it.

Through another dry sob, she says, "I love you more." I know she means it.

I clamp my teeth tight against my cheek and gnaw until I can focus on the coppery taste pooling in my mouth, grateful for the distraction. I throw on a clean change of clothes, charge down the hallway, and head out the door before I can be tempted to stick around and see how long it takes her to leave.

Keys slip between my slick fingers, and I struggle to start my car. My brain fixates on how to tell the doctor what happened *but not what really happened* and I yank the key back out. I sit in silence for a few minutes, maybe more, hoping it will allow her enough time to relax back into wherever she came from. I wrap the arms of an old hoodie around my arm and pull it tight, praying it will be enough to stop the blood. Feeling too exhausted and dizzy to try and start my car again, I head inside.

It's quiet. The house feels achingly empty, and I know I'm alone. I hate that I'm alone. As I head into the kitchen, I catch sight of the shimmering, bloodied scalpel. Without thinking, I scoop it up and head for the trash. Moldy grapes and the sour smell of crusted SpaghettiOs overwhelm my senses as I will myself to release the scalpel, but I'm too pathetic to let it go.

"Shit!" I yell in desperation.

I open the fridge and search for the only thing that sounds good when nothing else does: mother's homemade pickles. I don't care how long they've been sitting there. I yank a jar from the shelf, hungrily twist off the lid, and shove a spear into my mouth. The acidic, garlicky crunch jolts a familiar response from my salivary glands, and I can't chew them fast enough. It's only when my hand reaches into a pool of empty brine that I realize I've eaten every single one.

I wish my mother hadn't stopped making them. I'm not sure how many jars I have left, and I'm not sure what I'll do if I find out this was the last one.

The bottle weighs heavily in my hand. With genetic impulse, I drop in the scalpel and watch as bits of blood swirl through the remaining juice. I know exactly where to put it.

Full Immersion

Tiffany Michelle Brown

Tiffany Michelle Brown (she/her) is a Los Angeles-based writer who once had a conversation with a ghost over a pumpkin beer. She is the author of How Lovely To Be a Woman: Stories and Poems *and co-host of the Horror in the Margins podcast. Her fiction and poetry have been featured in publications by Black Spot Books, Death Knell Press, Hungry Shadow Press, and the NoSleep Podcast.*

☙❧

The cork cleaves in two as I pry it from dark glass. Bark rains down into the bottle like sad confetti. I'm not surprised. The expensive pinot has languished in my wine fridge for far too long. Still, it feels like a betrayal. A dig from the universe, which has been relentless in its cruelty lately.

I pull a metal sieve from a kitchen drawer and place it over the wine decanter. The mesh won't catch all the debris, but it'll filter out the largest pieces. With shaking hands, I pour the wine. As the pinot breathes, I peer out the window to check on Jamie.

It rained last night, fat drops that transformed our dusty backyard into a pit of sludge. He loves when the ground goes soft. Relishes the mire and filth. A month ago, I would've rushed outside to berate my son. I would've demanded he climb out of the muck right this instant and march upstairs for a bath. Tonight, I simply watch as he contorts his naked body into impossible shapes—contracting, lengthening, contracting, lengthening. The articulation of his spine makes me shudder.

The wine should sit for at least another thirty minutes, but I don't have the patience for that. Not tonight. Warm spices coat my tongue. The wine is meant to be savored, but I find my reflection in the bottom of the glass three separate times before I come up for air. My blood warms. My fingers tingle.

"It's just a phase," his general practitioner had said. "Kids at this age have such big imaginations. I bet he'll believe he's an astronaut next week."

Intellectually, this seemed like a sound assessment. And yet, on the ride home, my stomach twisted into knots so intricate, I had to pull over the car and stumble along the shoulder of the highway until my lungs no longer burned with anxiety. When we finally made it home, I called the doctor's office and asked for a referral to a child behavioral psychologist.

♦

After an initial consultation, the child psychologist asked me to bring Jamie in for observation. We stared at him through the glass, me biting my nails, the doctor composed and steady, her hair twisted up into an elegant chignon. Jamie immediately peeled the clothing from his skin, revealing a body covered in oozing sores and Band-aids trying and failing to keep his wounds clean and closed.

I dropped my gaze to the hem of my shirt, embarrassed, both by Jamie's nudity and the state of his body. I was sure the psychologist thought he was being abused. I opened my mouth to apologize, to explain there was no need to call child services, because *I* hadn't done this to my child. The psychologist intervened, placing her hand reassuringly on my forearm. If she had any concerns about my parenting, it was clear we would discuss them later.

In my periphery, the shadow of my son lowered himself to the low-pile carpet and began moving in circles through the playroom. Contract, lengthen, contract, lengthen.

⚭

I'm terrified this is all my fault. A little over a month ago, we were in Jamie's room after dinner pretending to be all manner of animals. First, we were pandas, tumbling around the room like balls of dough. Then lions, jumping, roaring, holding ourselves up with pride in our hearts. Flamingos balancing on one leg. Quokkas grinning. Worms slithering around the room on our bellies.

I called out hyena next, pushing my body up to all fours and erupting in deep-throated cackles, but Jamie refused to move from his prone position on the floor. He kept sliding across the carpet, balancing the weight of his little-boy body on his chin. I could see his skin turning an angry red, rugburn blossoming on his face.

"Possum," I shouted, collapsing on my back, playing dead. But Jamie kept inching toward me, his gaze fixed on mine, an eerie emptiness behind his eyes. His tongue lolled out of his mouth, dragging along the carpet, collecting hair and dirt and dust.

In a panic, I yanked him from the ground. "Playtime's over," I said. "Go brush your teeth." I gave him a nudge into the hallway. Jamie lowered himself to all fours and crawled to the bathroom. I didn't breathe until I heard water gushing from the faucet.

At bedtime, I rubbed Aquaphor into his rug-burned chin and kissed him goodnight. I hoped he'd return to normal in the morning.

But he hasn't. He's entirely mute. I can't keep clothes on him. He sneaks out to the backyard to roll around in the dirt. And that vacant chasm behind his eyes remains.

⁂

After observing Jamie for a good ten minutes, the psychologist offered me a practiced, too-optimistic smile. "We'll get to the bottom of this, Ms. Danforth. Do you mind if I go talk to him?"

I nodded, but I knew talking wouldn't get her anywhere. I was right. Jamie ignored the psychologist completely, continuing to creep around the room close to the water-stained baseboards.

The psychologist returned, her white smile still in place. "I know it's going to sound counterintuitive, but for a case like this, radical acceptance is your best bet. Any sort of opposition to his delusion will only encourage rebellion. While his behavior may seem extreme, I don't think you have anything to worry about. Simply go with it and see if anything changes. If it doesn't, we can, of course, discuss additional modes of treatment."

Before we left the office, the psychologist let me know she'd put in a call to our family doctor. She thought Jamie could benefit from some kind of topical antibiotic, perhaps something with steroids, to treat his brutalized skin.

⁂

I've done as directed—and more. I've delayed Jamie's enrollment in first grade despite having to forfeit the down payment to reserve his spot at the fancy parochial school I've always believed would foster his education and development. I've called his father, trying to enlist his help, but it's been years since we've talked, and his number is disconnected. Groceries are delivered once a week directly to our door so I don't have to leave Jamie on his own. A sitter is out of the question. I'm not sure I could pay a teenager enough to roll with my son's unique needs. I'm working from home indefinitely. I told my boss my son has a medical condition that will eventually resolve, but in the meantime, he needs my constant presence and care. I hired a handyman to extend our backyard fence further into the sky to give Jamie greater privacy when he's out back. I ignore the stares from our neighbors when I leave the house.

And I've begun researching earthworms in an effort to better understand Jamie. Try to connect with him. Continue to be his mother, any way that I can.

In an effort to keep him eating, I began keeping a plate piled high with spinach leaves, herbs, and mushrooms in the middle of the living room, knowing Jamie would graze throughout the day. I learned to leave the greens out on the counter so they had an opportunity to wilt, grow soupy, give off an unappetizing odor. The smell seemed to conjure my son. I'd plug my nose and watch him dive face-first into his plate, smudging his cheeks with slime.

One afternoon, I found him in the shed in the backyard, bent over a bag of gardening manure, munching away. My maternal instincts kicked in, and I screamed at him out of fear. I ordered him inside, but he wouldn't even acknowledge my presence. He ignored my every word. Kept chewing, shit caking his skin, jaw working the mixture into a brown, wet slurry.

I carried Jamie upstairs and cried for an hour as I scrubbed the filth from his body with soap and water. I kept asking him why he was doing this, why he'd eat manure, why he couldn't just be a normal little boy. Of course, I never received an answer.

I was terrified to call anyone for help—I really didn't need

CPS showing up at my door—so I watched him carefully the rest of the day. I waited for him to double over and vomit or show signs of weakening, but these symptoms never manifested. Jamie continued to shuffle along the carpet, leaving discarded Band-aids and scabbed skin in his wake, which I quickly sucked up with a hand-held vacuum cleaner. He spent the afternoon in the backyard, inching along the sun-warmed patio, snoozing in the uncut grass. He never so much as coughed. He seemed completely at peace.

I locked him in his bedroom that night, exhausted from standing sentinel all day and still very much on edge. Jamie hadn't shown any outward signs of poisoning, but could he experience a delayed reaction? Surely, he would've already shown signs of distress by now, right?

I laid in bed, imagining Jamie gasping for breath, losing motor function, collapsing beneath his Paw Patrol bed sheets. But each time I crept down the hall and peeked into Jamie's room, he was very much alive, gazing blankly at the ceiling, undulating like a wave.

The next day, Jamie was more energetic than usual. He gave off an air of strength and contentedness. His skin seemed to glow with vitality. The only difference in our daily routine had been his manure snack.

I realized I'd been going about his diet all wrong. I've started collecting fresh grass and half-decayed leaves from the backyard for Jamie's grazing dish. I sprinkle manure over the top like crumbled cheese on a salad. And it works. He spends more time in the living room with me each day, and the increased physical proximity gives me hope.

And yet…

It's been months. Months of radical acceptance. Of changing every aspect of our lives and trying to cater to his new predilections.

There's still a wall between us, an unseen force that continues to pull us further and further from each other. When I look at him, I still see my son. When he looks at me, I'm not sure if he sees anything.

♋

It feels like there's a storm brewing. The air hugs my body like water, tickling my calves and creeping beneath the plush material of my bathrobe. My brain feels gummy thanks to the wine, and I'm grateful. The liquor served its purpose. The less I think about what I'm about to do, the better.

Jamie winds his mud-caked body around the trunk of our lime tree. I watch him for a moment, studying how he moves, the ripple of energy that propels him steadily forward. My heart clenches. I miss my boy.

I close my eyes and concentrate on the hum of my blood as I untie my robe. My skin lights up with sensation as I lower myself to my belly. Cold mud immediately leeches to my body. Blades of grass press against me like the dull blade of a knife. I tremble, and tears threaten to spill over my cheeks.

The world looks different from the ground, overwhelming and vast and indistinct. A flicker of light green in my periphery gives me purpose. The lime tree. Jamie.

I try to move my body the way my son does, but no amount of hot yoga could have prepared me for the task. I flail and sweat and toss my torso around. I can feel bruises bloom beneath my skin. Cuts open up across my soft flesh. I smack my chin on the ground multiple times, and the taste of copper fills my mouth.

It feels like cheating, but I resort to using my arms to pull my body forward. My legs remain limp, pinned together by sheer will. Jamie needs to see my effort, my willingness to meet him in the mire, no matter how difficult, how painful.

I don't know how long it takes to get to the lime tree, but when I do, my body is spent. My arm muscles feel like frayed string cheese, and a primal cocktail of muck and blood covers every inch of my skin. I collapse, my chin sinking into soft earth, my lungs screaming for oxygen.

But it's all worth it, because my boy has waited for me. He stayed put, watched his mom work through the soil and shit and agony to be with him.

I know worms don't speak and this should be an exercise in full immersion, but his name bubbles up in my throat and can't be contained. "Jamie."

For the first time in weeks, recognition skitters across my son's features. There's something there behind his eyes. A warmth I convince myself could be love.

There's a flash of light, the crack of thunder, and then the rain comes.

To Cherish

SJ Townend

SJ Townend, an author of dark fiction, has stories published in a few places including with Ghost Orchid Press, Dark Matter Magazine, and Vastarien literary magazine. Her debut collection of unnerving short stories, Sick Girl Screams, is to be published by Brigid's Gate Press Oct' 2024 and her first romance novel, Pick-Up Lines, is set for publication with Champagne Book Group Spring/Summer 2024. You'll find her chasing her cat around the house, lurking on Twitter:@ SJTownend or hiding behind that sentinel oak in the woods.

CR80

He was desperate to know where the nearly-babies came from and the girl with the long, tangled plaits and the chipped front tooth said she knew. The girl, his neighbour, had been right about all the other things they'd discussed in the dark in the shared outdoor space between their neglected homes, like how the sun would never come out again, so he figured he had no reason not to believe her about the location of the babes.

Since way before the start of dark summer, the wood-skinned babes had appeared as glowing crops around the countryside, drawing people close with their infantile siren cries. Finding one of these bundles of half-alive joy had been all the boy had thought about since his mother had brought hers home: something to hold, something to cherish. An obsession.

◈

"Everyone has been paired up. The whole village has disappeared, must've found their babes and nested up. A done deal," the boy said to the girl.

"Everyone has received one, it appears, except for us," the snaggle-toothed girl replied. "Is it perhaps because we aren't good enough?"

"I have no idea," he said. He shrugged. But in his heart he felt she might once again be right.

The cobbled streets, usually flooded with the aroma of freshly baked bread and the choral mumblings of ale-addled farmers and a-throng with bustling villagers, had been empty, felt deserted for days. The bakers and the inn were now closed and Mr. Nevis, the postman with the oiled ginger curls who whistled his own familiar yet songless tune, had stopped delivering post a month back. Mr. Nevis had been the last person the boy had spoken to in any depth other than his mother, who was now lost, and his neighbour.

"Come," the girl said. "Let's get moving." She shone her torch on the cart by her feet. "If we find a birthing spot, we can pull more babes back in this."

"Makes sense," said the boy.

"I'm sure the map will take us straight to the source."

He wondered what she'd be like as a mother, this girl he'd known for all eleven years of his life, his neighbour. At only a year and a month older than him, he wasn't sure she'd be any good at caring for something so small, so helpless, especially with the shortage of sunshine and the many challenges that brought. He certainly felt he wasn't ready for parenthood, but he didn't feel he had a choice. "We've got to find them," he said. "They'll be orphaned without us. No one will save them, activate them, because everyone in the village is already busy, present yet vacant, with theirs."

To be an orphan meant no parents, no grown-up to tuck you in at night and kiss you on the forehead and slice up an apple into neat segments. The boy had found cutting up and preparing his own food a challenge. The sharp knife his mother had never let him use before had hurt when his fingers had slipped and received its wrath the night before. Orphaned was exactly how he'd felt since his mother had become preoccupied with her new nearly-baby. The boy sighed. The warmth of his exhalation hung in the otherwise silent black air between the two children for a short moment. He wanted to ask her if she felt the same, unloved, unlovable, but decided to change the subject. She could change her mind about all of it, their desperate quest, if he became emotional. "Do you think they're airlifted in from somewhere? And if so, by who?" he said. "And why?"

"Does it really matter how they get here?" The girl's words came quick and hard, each an angry blow to the boy's confidence. "Once you hold one in your arms, and it softens into you, you'll not care for anything else."

The thought of this brought a smile to the boy's lips, but the girl did not see because her torch was not pointing the right way and for several months, their village had been immersed in a blanket of darkness. But the boy wanted to express his happiness to her, so he took her free hand and guided it towards his balled cheeks. "You're excited," she said, a statement, not a question. "Me too." She pulled her hand away and reached down for the cart rope which lay on the ground by her feet. "Come on. The sooner we find them, the sooner we can hold them."

"But," the boy shifted his weight from left foot to right, "seriously, don't you ever even consider where they come from?"

"Oh, I don't know. Maybe someone from another village just turns up with a truckload. Your guess is as good as mine. But we have a map, so I guess we just call it a blessing and be grateful. Part of me thought we'd missed the boat." She shone her torch on his shoes and then let the triangle of white light fall on the dark path in front of them again. "Come," she said.

"Coming." He began to march after her. Adrenaline quick-silvered through his veins at the thought of what they might find.

They marched in silence through the dark of the day until the silence was broken by the girl. She stopped to speak. "If we do find the nearly-babies—*when* we find them—we take as many as we can manage and give them all the love we have," she said.

"I guess," he mumbled. "I mean, I'd like to think that's what will happen. I have so much love to give, and no one else to give it to right now—" She began to stride forwards again with a renewed zest. Her feet made a *pit pat* sound on the firm mud and grass. He followed the girl, unsure as to whether he should offer to tow the empty cart up the dirt track away from the girl's father's hay barn where they'd met, or let her struggle onwards. "W-would—"

She stopped again and, this time, turned around. With the torch in her hand, she illuminated her face as if about to whisper a ghost story around a campfire. She groaned. "What is it? Spit it out."

"Doesn't matter."

"Listen. They probably die, the babies, if you don't give them enough love. You know that, right?" she said. "The nearly-babes might die. If they're unloved, not held when they cry after they've been activated, we will have nothing left to hold and feed. And we can't let them die. We can't let anyone else get there first."

"There's nothing I'd like more than to hold one, nurture it for as long as it'll let me," the boy said. He bunched his fists into his pockets. He could just about make out the outline of a pebble by his foot under the light of the girl's torch. He kicked it away from the path. "I can't remember what it feels like to hold another breathing thing close. My mother hasn't touched me for weeks. I haven't seen another soul other than you in months." He sighed.

The girl flashed the beam in his eyes. "You and me both, bud. But don't go getting any ideas. And keep your greasy mitts off me." She dropped the rope of the cart, stepped towards him, and pointed to her upper middle cracked tooth. She moved in closer, so close he could smell the lack of care on her breath. He held his breath and turned his face away from hers. "This was how my father showed me love before him and my mother left with their new ones. Good riddance to parents, I say. Neither of them had time for me anyway, especially after their nearly-babies arrived. My father didn't even take his beloved whisky bottles with him."

The girl knocked into the cart as she spoke and the cart began to trundle back down the slope. The boy stopped it with the side of his shin. He held in a yelp as the jagged wooden corner scraped against his leg.

"I know," he replied. "And I'm sorry. If it's any consolation, I haven't seen my mother since she got hers either. She hasn't even spoken to me. She took her nearly-baby from the delivery man before I could even see it, let alone hold it, and now the only sound she makes is with her fist against her bedroom wall. She bangs and bangs on the wall until I slide her in bread and milk."

"Sucks to be you."

"I remember it crying once, the baby. Its screeching woke me on the fourth or fifth night after it arrived. It cried for ages, and then it stopped. There was peace for a moment until Mother screamed. I haven't heard it cry since and ever since, Mother hasn't left her bedroom."

"Oh, the sound of a nearly-baby's crying is the worst. I guess."

"Yes. Yes it is."

The pair continued to walk.

❧

"I think we're at the final crossroads," the girl said. She waved the beam of light ahead of them. The weak light bounced back: the tree they used to hang a rope swing from and play, before the darkness came, a sentinel oak bent like an old maid with a dowager's hump. "Yes, this is it. We're close."

The girl stopped and pulled out a folded sheet from the pocket of her dungaree dress. With three shakes, the map was open. She directed the torch beam onto the tatty paper and traced the route they'd need to take with her fingertip.

"The map," he asked. "You say the storekeeper gave it to you then ran back upstairs?"

"Correct. He'd said he was out of stock, said he was tired, and asked if I was certain it was what I wanted, a nearly-baby," the girl said. "I visited his store every day for a fortnight, travelled there by torchlight, stubbed my toes on the journey more times than I care to remember."

"Paid off though, I guess," the boy said.

"I kept visiting, asking if he was expecting any more in. He must've grown tired of me bothering him. I'd ring the bell and each time he'd come down the stairs. No lights at all. No idea if he even had any clothes on or not. His stale smell filled the shop floor."

"Ew."

"He snapped at me every time I called, said I'd wake his baby if I carried on ringing the bell. But I guess you're right. My persistence did pay off."

"Because he gave you the directions."

"Correct."

"And here we are," the boy said.

"And here we are." The girl passed the torch to the boy. "Here, hold this. I think I know where to go now." She folded up the map and slid it back in her pocket. The torch flickered and dimmed in the boy's hand. "Dammit. It's running out." She took the torch back and pulled out new batteries from the satchel she wore over her body and replaced them. "Last lot," she said.

"Oh," the boy replied. "Guess we better get moving."

"Onwards. Into the woods."

They walked for another mile or so, around and through fields, until they reached the edge of the forest.

"Is it odd to not feel scared?" the boy said. "Or not as scared as I did when I came here once last year, before the sun went? In the dark, the forest feels the same as anywhere else."

"What you can't see can't scare you."

"You think? It's so quiet, as if all the wildlife has gone too," he said.

"Probably has. Nothing grows well without sunlight."

The boy shuddered. "Well, it's certainly colder," he replied.

She agreed. Wrapped in perpetual darkness, the woods were

no different than the rest of the village in which they resid-ed. Bathed in black, they could not tell with their eyes where the field ended and where the thickness of trees began. Only with their hands and feet, it became apparent. "Come closer, so you don't stumble, the ground is uneven here, covered with some sort of bracken and darned twisted roots," she said. She dropped the tow rope of the cart and linked her arm through his. "We'll leave the cart here."

They didn't have to walk far until they heard the melody. "The babies are near," she said. "What a song. If all the black keys on the upright piano in the school hall were played in turn, softly, in an order never attempted before by any human, it wouldn't match the beauty of this music."

"It's…enchanting," he whispered.

The girl stopped and squeezed the boy into her side a little closer. "But they never sing as sweetly again as they do before you hold them for the first time," she said. "Molly told me so. Before her father bought her one from the black market and she stopped coming to school."

Hand in hand, the two children crept towards the music, until a cluster of emerald eyes winking through the blanket of blackness brought them both to a standstill. "Have you ever seen such a beautiful shade of green?" she said and dropped the boy's hand. He was lost for words. She shone the torch beam onto the collection of babes and the melody escalat-ed into high pitched screams. "Crikey," she said. "Sorry." He grabbed her torch and angled its beam towards the forest floor. The melody became pleasant again so the girl and the boy edged towards the thumbprint swirl of blinking green lights.

"Like wood," he said. His sentence came out incomplete.

"Yes, they are. Their skin, it's like knotted, polished timber—until you activate them."

The volume of the nearly-babies increased as the girl passed the torch to the boy. "Here, take it," she said. He took the flashlight and she crouched down and lifted a singing babe up in her arms.

"You're so cold. There, there, my darling." She whispered into where its ear would form.

The boy placed the torch on the forest floor and followed suit, taking hold of the babe nearest him. "There, there."

"This is unreal," she said quietly. "I never thought I'd get my own, and here we are. There are four, five including the one you're holding. All mine."

"Ours," he said.

"Yes. You can take one, these four need me."

He ran his fingertips over the nearly-babe's hard outer casing. The green eye-lights twinkled like the stars the two children used to lie on the roof of the barn and gaze at.

"A true blessing. Those who wait the longest receive the most," she whispered. She placed and held her forefinger over each green eye of the babe in the crook of her arm until the eyes no longer glowed. If it weren't for the dim circle of yellow the flashlight yielded, the girl and the babe would have sunken into the darkness of the wood completely. "Go ahead," she said, "activate yours too." The boy did as instructed. The girl held her babe close to her chest and then gathered up the others. Two were strewn on the forest floor and one was propped upright against a tree trunk. She held each close and activated it with her fingertip, then kissed each on where its forehead would develop.

As the last pair of green eye-lights went out, the sweet harmony stopped. The sound of their own breathing and the occasional crunch of leaf litter underfoot as they moved was all the two children could hear.

The boy picked up the torch from the ground, careful to support the fragile head of his baby as he did so. "I feel like a God," the girl said.

"A creator," the boy said. "They're so small. My heart might pop."

"The four of them together, I never knew I could feel so joyful," she said. "But my, they are weighty for their size. I daren't put them down." The girl rose up and took the boy's hand and together, they walked back out of the forest towards where they'd left the cart.

"Let's leave the cart. Unless you want to use it?" she said. "We should head back to the barn and rest there until we've enough energy to take them back to our homes."

The wood-like skin of his babe had already started to soften, become more flesh-like. Undulating fronds where he presumed arm buds might swell tickled against his skin. "No. I don't want to use the cart. I never want to put this one down."

"I feel them softening," she said. "They're gaining in weight too, already. I want to place them on my skin. Need to. But not here, not in the forest. It's too cold."

"Here," he said. He stretched out his arm. "Let me take one or two of yours. I can carry more weight. Just until we get back to the barn."

Before he had a chance to touch one of the four babies in her arms, she snarled. The boy gasped. "Back off. Not a chance. These are mine. My babies. I got the map. So I get the lion's share."

"Sure," the boy said. He recoiled. "I'm sorry." He lifted his t-shirt up and placed his own baby against the skin of his chest. Instinct told him to do this. *Much easier to do with one than four,* he thought. He couldn't hold in the gasp of pure joy he felt as the wood began to moisten, soften off as it touched the smooth flesh of his chest. "One will be enough for me," he said. *Surely, one will be enough,* he thought. He'd never felt such ecstasy. Pure, unfettered, unfiltered adoration for another thing. How could he want for anything more?

"Spring meadows, lemon balm." The girl inhaled her catch deeply and swayed with the scent. One of the young in her arms wriggled, then whimpered. She was taken aback and stumbled slightly. It was the first sound any of the babies had made since their sweet melody had stopped. A flashback to the brick-laden bag of kittens her uncle had made her carry to the river several years ago. "That was…different," she said.

"We must get going," the girl said, and with four babies, each softening slightly in her arms, each moulding and contorting its wet willow limbs inwards and around her waist and chest to find its special place with its new mother, she turned to exit the forest. "Come on, I need you to shine the way." One of her yield released another uncomfortable murmur. She cooed. The soothing nature of her voice calmed the fidgeting bundle in her arms. She cooed all the walk back.

⚭

"Please, let me in." The boy rapped on the front door of the girl's house. He'd lost track of how many days it had been since their journey into the woods. He must have closed his eyes for a split second, exhausted from caring for his baby, and his babe, strapped to his chest with its own limb buds, had started to cry. He knocked again, harder. He needed to get into the warmth of the girl's house so he could unswaddle the baby in order to begin the tedious stroking ritual the little one demanded. He reached down and felt his leg gently. He'd tripped on his way, in the dark, to the girl's house, despite its proximity to his. The graze on his knee burnt.

Caring for the baby was hard enough, despite the lack of light. His mother had taken the last of the candles into her room before she took up residence there. The boy had reached breaking point, alone in the dark with the fresh wood-baby, so he left his house to the sound of his mother banging the wall of her bedroom. This was her demand for food, but there was nothing left in the kitchen to give her and he had spiked his hand hard on a broken glass jar while rummaging in the back of the larder.

His decision to head over to the girl's house had not come easy—he was a little afraid of how she would react to his neediness—but he wanted to know what he had witnessed was normal, and he wanted to find out the best way to cope. And the girl next door always had answers.

"Get in." The girl opened the door. A row of candles on a plinth in her hallway flickered and rippled with the draft as she did so. He squinted at the brightness of her entrance room. "You look how I feel," he said.

"Exhausted?" she replied. "I haven't slept for days, not since we got back from the barn."

"Same." The boy followed the girl through. Despite the weariness he felt, despite questioning his own sanity at times, to be in her presence, in the presence of another not made from softened wood or cursed with the piercing cry of a banshee, was what he needed. And to be in a room with light again, after so long in the darkness of his own abode, felt better. He exhaled audibly and she waved him through to her living room where he sank into a wicker cup chair.

"Here. Breakfast." The girl passed him a muffin. "It's stale but it's sustenance. The weight has fallen off you."

"Thank you. And same. I see your collarbone." He took a bite. His empty stomach curled with the arrival of the solid food. Slowly. He would need to eat it slowly in order to not vomit. He placed the cake down on a table at his side and began the laborious process of untying his baby from his chest.

"They don't come away easily, do they?" she said and lifted her shirt. The boy, for the first time, was glad at the dimness of the lighting. Myriad leather-like digits and limbs probed and hustled for skin space on the girl's bruised-blue torso. She stroked what he considered might be the spine of one of her babes and she cooed weakly. "There, there," she said. He turned away, unable to watch.

"No." He pried what he presumed were the lips of his nearly-babe from a raised mole on his stomach with the firm slip of his pinky and began to peel away the rest of the baby from his chest. The girl strode around the room, in a repeating circuit, caressing each of her young ones in turn.

"I want you to watch something," he said. "I need to know if this is happening to you too."

"Go ahead," she said. She turned to face the boy then continued to rock in rhythm with her own gentle cooing and hushing.

The boy laid his baby down flat on the edge of the rug which lay in between him and the girl. His near-babe began to whimper, then cry, then scream. The boy gripped the arms of his chair tightly. "I want to pick it up again. I've an overwhelming urge to tend to it, make it feel loved, safe, but I'm empty inside. Tired out. Every part of me aches. The lack of sleep, the constant soothing, it's too much." He spoke louder as the sound of his baby amplified.

"Make it stop," she shouted. Several of her babes, all strapped around her waist and sides, all in awkward positions, burst into tears. The boy's babe screamed louder. "I never let mine cry so loud," she snapped. Her eyes widened until, even in the dim light, the boy could see their whites.

"Please," he said, his hands clamped, prayer position in front of his chest. "Please, just wait."

The shrill sound from his baby grew and grew. Louder. Louder. Until it stopped. "Look," he said. "Its cheeks." His nearly-baby on the floor, part knotted-wood, part frilly pink-white tissue, inhaled deeply through the gash on its top half. The two children watched on as the babe's cheeks puffed out.

"What is it doing?" she said. "Help it!" She wrapped her arms tight around her own collection of babes and kissed each one on where its fully formed head would grow.

"This. This happened yesterday. I couldn't take any more, couldn't hold it any longer. Its suction slit found my nipples. Look at them!" The boy lifted his shirt up and moved towards the lamp at his side. The girl gasped. "They're red raw. I bled, it bit on me so hard. And believe me, I wanted to let it carry on, because, for a moment, it seemed content, at peace, but it hurt. It hurt so much." He dropped his shirt, buckled forward in his seat and cried.

"I don't know what to say. You just have to keep on loving it. Love it with all you have in your heart. You can do it. What do they say, the days are long but the years are short." She paused and prized away one of her own babe's wooden spindles which had begun to search upwards for her breast. "Ouch. And they won't be babies forever." She reached forward and patted the boy on the knee, then brushed her hand against his face, wiping a tear from his cheek.

"I know. I'm trying. Believe me. It fills me with an unmatchable happiness when it eventually pulls its roots out from my flesh and unclamps its slit and dozes against my skin. But I'm so tired. I swear I'm delusional. That's why I came here. I need you to see this too."

"The breath-holding?" The girl tilted her head, looked down at the baby on the floor. "It must be some sort of protest. It's unhappy you've removed it and placed it on the floor, surely. Who can blame it?"

"Yes. That may well be the case. But that's not all, the breath-holding," he said. "Watch." He gestured with a limp wrist and pointed finger at his babe on the floor without looking up. "Please."

She crouched down by the side of his baby, drew her nose closer to the now tight slit at the top of the bundle of knots and softness, and observed.

"It's turning blue," she said, flustered. "I need to pick it up, please, let me touch your child. This is unbearable, watching it puff out its cheeks like this. I swear, the place where its face will form is swelling, growing. Its unhappiness is unsettling my babes. My youngest is arching." She pointed to the baby draped over her left shoulder. "And this one here, on my hip, the first one I activated, its writhing, pulsing almost, like it feels the pain of yours. You can't leave yours here on the ground. Please, before it attaches—pick it up. Look—it's putting out roots into the floorboards, see?"

"Please, be patient. Place your fingers in your ears, coo. Just wait and watch."

But she couldn't resist helping it. Mother's instinct. With a gentle hand, she caressed the side of part of its top. The roots the babe had laid down flash-recoiled and the girl yanked her hand away in shock and fell back. The nearly-babe on the floor opened up its slit and sucked in a large volume of air through its pre-mouth gash. The babe swelled up more, inflated. Its barky flesh stretched and widened, and it became globular in shape until the whole babe had tripled in size.

"Please, pick it up," she said. "It won't let me touch it." Her finger stung where she had tried to soothe the boy's babe.

"Just watch," the boy said. He was not watching. His face was firmly planted in the palms of his hands.

His babe slowly lifted off from the ground, until eventually no part of it touched the rug or the floor boards. "It's floating," she screamed. Her babies matched her volume. She ran out into the hallway.

The boy looked up. *It wasn't a delusion,* he thought. *They float.* The baby's cheek pads puffed out further and further and it rose up like a light balloon until it hovered midway between the floor and the ceiling. "Look at its skin. Gone blue," he said. "When you ignore them, leave them to cry, they hold their breath until they float. I just needed someone else to witness it, to know I'm not going mad."

"Just take it back into your arms, where it's supposed to be," she yelled. "Please. Take it back or get out."

"Yes. Of course. You're right. I need to hold it again. That feeling when they sleep on your chest. Nothing beats it." The boy sprung up then he just stood statuesque, as if tethered to the spot. "But I'm so tired of holding it. Alone in that dark house, with no food, with what might as well be the ghost of my mother banging on her bedroom wall, giving all her love to another bundle. Who holds me, who soothes me?"

"Your nearly-baby gives you all the love you'll ever need," she said. "The slit, take it and angle the slit on your nipple again, please. Breathe through the discomfort. Endless giving, it's what a parent should do for their baby, in return for unconditional love."

"But it's not my baby," he whispered. Quietly enough for her not to hear. "It's not even a baby." He looked to his feet then walked slowly towards the door.

"You can't leave it with me, I have four of my own, they

give me all I need. I've nothing left to give another. Besides, yours won't even let me touch it." The girl marched towards the boy and pushed in front of him, her weak body working as a shield to the door to block him from leaving.

"And I need light. I can't bear to live in darkness any longer. You have so much light here and I have nothing." The boy seized the opportunity and grabbed a lantern from the cabinet by the girl's front door.

"If you're not going to love it, at least take it with you. Please don't leave it here, it takes up so much space. And what if it stops holding its breath and starts to cry again? Please, take it away with you." The girl lurched forwards, away from the door, and grabbed the floating nearly-babe by one of its unfurled limbs. "Please take it away." The boy pushed past her, towards the open door and stepped outside. The girl pushed his baby after him but he refused to hold onto it.

The boy's baby opened up its slit and took in a large gasp of air and grew larger. The skin which held it together stretched out so thin, it became translucent in patches. A muffled blue hue shone from within it which illuminated it.

"That's new," the boy said. He pointed at his baby. "That light within it." A pang of fresh love struck his heart and he reached out, shoulder height, to touch his baby. "Perhaps I can tolerate it a little longer. Maybe it will get easier to care for as it grows." The blue light within the baby flickered off and on and off and on. The boy grappled after it, jumped and tried to reach for it back, but in a matter of seconds, the ball of near-ly-baby had risen up higher and became out of his reach.

Too high. It floated upwards, far far out of his reach. It drifted out of the door and rose up and out of the girl's house. As it came into contact with the cool external air, the blue light within the baby disappeared completely. Much like the sun had all those months ago. But the boy and the girl could still see the baby, despite the darkness. Its taut skin reflected the light of the lantern. The boy lifted the lantern and stood and watched as the babe-orb inhaled and inhaled, increased in diameter, and rose up and up.

The boy and the girl could make out its flailing oaky limbs which began to kick and bend and the nearly-baby swam up higher, into the dark sky.

With their necks flexed back, the children stared up until the boy's baby became a dot up in what, despite its hellish, lightless nature, must've been the morning summer sky. They squint-ed. The boy cried. A sadness greater than the dark sky which stretched above him yanked at his heart, pulled him to an even more bleak place than the Earth had become since the sun had appeared to have taken its final breath. A misery with more depth than the author sharing this tale with you may have felt, when perchance, once she herself had become embalmed with the despair of watching on helpless, as her nearly-babe took one final breath in her arms and never a second.

The girl cried too. "Angle the lantern in such a way so we can see your baby," she said through sobs. They watched up, up, as it drifted further from her house. The girl gasped. "Look," she said, her voice louder.

The boy's baby, a small orb reflecting the light of the lan-tern in an otherwise black landscape, bumped into another small flailing-limbed ball. Both children squinted. "Another inflated baby," the girl said. "I can make out your nearly-babe, there," she pointed with the lantern in her outstretched arm, "and another baby there, see, at its side." And she was correct. They watched on in awe as the boy's babe nudged anoth-er baby, which Newton's cradled a cluster of other inflated, wood-skinned balls.

The two children shrieked. A sharp beam of sunlight broke through the blackness and singed the children's retinas, as the bunch of floating babies rippled to the side. The boy closed his eyes. A staggered rainbow of the outline of his own darling inflated baby imprinted onto the inside of his eyelid.

"The sun," he said, his voice reedy, desperate, dry with exhaustion. He rubbed his eyes then opened them again. "Up there. In front of the sun, the darkness is nothing but a thick cloud of inflated nearly-babies, lifting upwards, towards the heavens."

In a split second, the sunshine burst disappeared, became clouded over again, and, as if on cue, the lantern supped up the last of its kerosene and dipped out. Side by side, the boy and the girl and everything else in existence became immersed once more in darkness, lost to the eternal heartbreak of the midnight of summer.

On her breast, one of the girl's nearly-babies began to stir, de-latched, and opened up wide its feeding slit. Despite the girl's efforts to soothe it, it broke into a cry, a piercing howl. With the cup of her hand, the girl clasped the place where she worried the full head of her babe might soon form. On the spot, she rocked slightly, a little broken, the way new mothers do when immersed with what seems like the forevermore, when soothing a precious one, the one they love yet fear. "There, there," she said, knowing not what else to say. She placed her lantern on the ground and with her spare hand, she reached across and fumbled in the darkness until she found him. She patted the crown of the head of the weeping boy. On the long, unseen grass outside of the house in which the girl would spend the rest of her life, the boy had fallen to his knees. His face once more pressed into his palms. "There, there."

Grotesque

Allison Wall

Allison Wall is a queer, neurodivergent writer whose work explores deconstruction, self-discovery, and belonging. She has an MFA in Creative Writing from Hamline University. Her short fiction has appeared in Electric Spec, Crow & Cross Keys, *and* NonBinary Review, *among others. Allison is present (if not active) on social media sites as @awritingwall, and you can find her on her website, <u>allison-wall.com</u>, where she occasionally blogs about things like the intersection of neurodivergence and surrealist art.*

◌৪৪০

When I woke, I was made of skin and bones, meat and gristle. I don't know what woke me. Maybe it was the granite melting, or else cracking like a shell, to fall, and scatter on the street below. I don't know where the stone went, or how long I had been transformed. I knew only my immediate physical sensations—new, insistent.

It was raining. Pouring. Waterfalls of city rain. And with those watery darts, I was cold for the first time. Stone doesn't feel cold. Stone absorbs warmth and imparts coldness. Now, being flesh, being cold, my skin prickled. I shivered.

I turned my head on my neck, my neck on my shoulders, my shoulders on my spine. Tendons and bone ground together. Every muscle ached. Was it the movement? Or the decades of non-movement prior? In any case, I could see no evidence of what had caused this change to my body. No one else was on the roof—no one of flesh, that is. My siblings still sat, crouched and stone upon their plinths. They kept watch, as they always had, over the gutters and the ledges, over the height and the drop. How they leered, and with what marvelous ferocity! I alone had been transformed. I alone felt pain.

My mind, which had only ever moved its stone pace, was speeding up. Electricity zipped through me. I had felt electricity before: the rare lightning strike. That was a tickle; this was a dreadful rush, a clattering of sensation, a mighty push to *move*, to *do*.

Moving, doing: never had I attempted such things! Stone exists. That is enough. But this body demanded more. Gravity afflicted me, from the tip of my head to the soles of my feet, compressing. Wind and rain whipped ice through my veins. I could not remain so exposed.

There was a shelter on the rooftop. I had never seen it before, because of the direction I had been faced. Carefully, I went to it. Stone is solid. Flesh is a dance of tensions and releases. Pains in my ankles and knees, hips popping, vertebrae settling, ribs shifting. How could skin be strong enough to contain these internal workings?

The shelter had an opening, and I went through, into the building I had guarded but never entered. Within was a pit, bordered by ground that descended in a measured way. By putting one foot carefully upon the next depression and then the next, I could go down the vertical length of the pit safely. I had to turn my clawed feet sideways to manage, which caused strain upon my ankles. The first door I saw, I went through, though I did not know where it might lead.

I found myself in a white space, completely shut off from the sky and wind. Then, from a distance, I heard a noise. No, not a noise, for noise implies cacophony. This was intentional: sound, but more than sound. It rolled in warm tones—not that the tones were physically warm, but they put into my chest a sensation of comfort.

I perked my ears and stepped out into the huge space, hunting the sound. My claws scraped upon the shining floor, a most unpleasant sensation. I tried to mitigate this by mincing along. This was effective, but shortening my stride tightened the muscles in my legs painfully.

As I drew nearer, the sound changed: first emphatic, heraldic, plunging to something like darkness, then up again to warmth and light. The feelings inside me shifted, too. It was a kind of magic. Perhaps the sort that had transformed me atop the roof—that called me—that could cure me, if I appealed to it.

Then, came a different sound. Much closer. I had heard this sound before, though never so close. Human voices: those unnatural flesh sounds produced within the body, emanating from the wet cavity of the mouth. My stomach twisted, to hear them.

The voices approached, louder, echoing, so that I could not understand any single word. Finding a crevice, I hid myself, hoping these flesh creatures would pass me by. But I had not hidden well. Two human creatures stopped and looked at me. They were only as tall as my shoulder (not measuring the spikes).

"Woah," said one. "Hair and makeup is really killing it!"

The other reached toward me.

I recoiled from their touch.

"Sorry, right, I shouldn't fuck up your makeup."

The other peered up at me. "Damn, did they put you on stilts?"

"Are you wearing prosthetics too? I don't even recognize you. Who are you?"

The humans looked at me. Waiting for me to account for myself, somehow, among their confusion of words.

I had never spoken before. Never coordinated the noise of a wet throat with the movement of lips, teeth, sharp against the softness of my tongue. I feared that, if I should attempt speech, I would utter such sounds as would terrify them.

I pointed at my throat with a single claw, hoping to convey my difficulty.

"Oh, vocal rest."

They nodded.

"Take care of yourself. And break a leg!"

They showed their teeth at me and kept walking.

Break a leg? I thought I might do just that, so tight were my muscles. Could muscle snap a bone? Why would the human wish such a thing upon me? Perhaps they were rejecting me, or cursing me.

In my ribs, there was a fluttering weakness. It made my body feel too shallow for the air that moved in and out, in and out. It made a tapping from within. Not knowing what this might signify, I waited. Perhaps another transformation was imminent! But no. The sensation faded.

With no better goal, I continued hunting the sounds. I followed them, winding through shadowy places, before coming to the blackest doorway of all. Upon the other side was a stunning vibrance of light. Staring into the morning sun could not have been more blinding.

From thence came the sound. And I saw, upon the lighted platform, there were humans, many humans, who, all together, opened their mouths and added to the sound.

Such noises! Loud, louder than should have been possible, boisterous, bouncing, reverberating. The sound poured over me. The humans moved about the platform, some dancing, some gesturing with arms. The energy was magnetic. And I thought, if flesh bodies can perform this impossible feat, it is better to be flesh than stone! For stone is impenetrable, but stone is still. Stone cannot add to the noise of the universe. It is silent. Stone has strength in waiting. Better far, it seemed to me, to live one life in such a way, than to spend hundreds of them motionless and quiet atop a roof.

I longed—oh, how I longed!—to leap into the light and cavort with the humans. I edged nearer to the dividing line where light cut through the dark. I paid no heed to anything save the light, the mirth, the sound. It drew me.

"What are you doing?" hissed a voice at my side.

I turned, quick.

There was a person. A black wire wrapped over the top of their head. It extended to their mouth, though they were covering that part with their hand.

"I didn't call for demons. Hell isn't until Act Two."

I did not understand.

"Chorus isn't allowed to hang around backstage." The person wrinkled the skin of their face. Raised one arm, and at its end, extended a finger.

I followed the finger with my gaze to a hallway.

"Go."

So I followed the finger, moving gingerly, careful not to disturb any of the objects stacked, nor to tangle my horns in any of the ropes or fabric draping. The hall yielded to another descent, and down I went. In this movement the pain of my flesh body returned.

But I had forgotten it!

The glorious curtain of sound had swallowed up pain from my consciousness altogether. It had not healed me, for again I felt the stabbing in my knees, the ache of my ankles, the tightness of my hips; no, not healed, but it had turned my awareness from physical discomfort to something sublime. Caught up in such splendor, all pain had been washed clean. Perhaps if I could remain in that place of shadow and light—but I was not allowed. I had been forced to move on.

And where was I going? At the bottom of the descent, there was another hall, but in this one there was a great bustle. Bodies of flesh everywhere, too numerous and quick to count. Everywhere, voices echoing. The humans moved around me. They barely glanced at me. They thought I belonged to this bizarre activity. They assumed I had a place among these rituals, of which I understood nothing. They did not see how my once-stone body was twisting, being crushed. They did not see that I needed help.

I retreated from the maelstrom, pushed as by the street sweepers with their rotating brushes, into a dark room. I climbed behind a row of softness, hiding even deeper from sight. I curled myself upon the ground, closed my eyes, and imagined that I was turning back into stone. I was becoming once more hardened, confident in the structure of my body, a form that would bother no one, a form that would cause me no pain. This did not work.

The chaos of human activity ebbed and flowed and ebbed again. All was still. Time passed.

I tried to unmoor my mind, to drift, as I once had, among my dreams. Ah, yes, stone dreams: of misty highlands where mother mountain sleeps, of time immeasurable pressed into layers of sediment. Stone dreams the lives of the bones and minerals and creatures that compose it. Stone dreams of starlight drifting through void, when the distant past and the distant future join hands, encircling the place where a planet once spun, a farce of odds, a joke the universe told itself to pass a portion of infinity.

But I could not dream. I could not separate myself from this soft body's suffering. Every pulsation of my veins, every breath scraping down my throat, kept the time. My flesh measured it, every crumb. None escaped my notice.

Eventually, there came a rhythmic noise, a pigeon picking through pebbles. No. Footsteps. Click, click, upon a hard floor. A light burst bright upon my eyes. Beyond the wall of soft-hanging-things, someone moved. A human.

I felt fear. I lay rigid upon the hard ground.

They made some noises, like wind blowing around a corner, and then—something else. It was like the fantastical sounds that had drawn me before. Like and unlike: a singular part, rather than a glorious whole. Quiet, gentle, the sound ran down, flowing, in a pattern. The pattern was repeated over and over, rising, like the song of a finch.

Thus enchanted, and with my muscles threatening spasm, I emerged from the soft hangings.

The human looked at me where I crouched upon the floor. They said, "Oh my god!"

I reached out a claw, hoping to convey friendliness, harmlessness, my desire for them to continue their birdsong.

The human flinched. Movement caught my eyes. I looked, and I saw the room reflected, shining, from a plate upon the wall. I was there, and so was the human. I straightened my frame carefully, joints popping, and I was much taller than they. Apart from the general structure of four limbs, torso, and head, we looked very little alike. I had horns, a hooked nose, claws, tail, a mottled coloration of rough skinflesh. My teeth were pointed, and my skeleton boasted extra bones: spiked protrusions, most fearsome and majestic.

"Are you going to hurt me?" they asked.

Compared to such a small creature, with hardly any teeth, with no spikes or claws at all, I must have been frightening, though I could not have attacked them, not with the pain in my body. I had to risk speech to reassure them.

Carefully, I formed the word, putting the tip of my tongue just so behind my top teeth, and whispered, "No."

I feared the sound of my voice: that it would be gravel and flint, but it was not. It had a surprising melodic tone. The pressure of it in my throat was discomfiting, however, and I did not like the sensation. It was like something caught there was straining to get out.

The human's face skin wrinkled. "Why are you in my dressing room?"

"Hiding."

"From what?"

A good query! I had established no enemies among the humans. Perhaps I had been hiding from myself, or from the nightmare my reality had become. This was too much to put into speech.

The creature's eyes moved over my body. "You're not wearing makeup, are you?"

I looked at them, unsure.

They took a bright white square and held it over my arm. "Can I?"

I waited in acquiescence.

They swiped the cloth across my flesh. It was cool. Refreshing. It came away as white as it had been.

The human dropped it. "What are you?"

Here, at last, was a creature who discerned my difference. A warm wave pushed upward past my throat and into my eyes. They became wet. My vision blurred. I lost orientation with the room, lost balance, and stumbled upon a sore knee.

The human touched my arms. Steadied me. The wrinkles in their face skin changed, and when they spoke again, the same question, their voice was softer.

"I became flesh, and it was raining. So I came inside."

"You *became* flesh?" asked the human. "Were you something else before?"

"Stone."

"Where did you come from?"

"Roof."

"Will you show me?"

I limped to the hall, feeling keenly what a poor choice it had been, to have lain upon the ground for so long. I feared the climb, but the human directed me to something called an elevator: a metal box that lifted us up. The pressure was terribly strange; even after we got out, the earth was moving beneath me and my head threatened to float away. I put my hand on top to keep it secure.

On the roof, it was early afternoon, and the sun was shining. There was my plinth. An empty space that I had once filled. My siblings were all there, still stone. None of them had transformed in my absence.

"Holy shit," said the human. "You're a gargoyle."

"Gar. Goyle." This word, a horrific sensation in the undulating confines of my throat.

"Wait. I learned about this when I was studying in Paris. If you have a water spout, you're a gargoyle. If you don't, you're a grotesque." The human peered at my siblings. "These don't have spouts. So, grotesque."

"Grotesque." More graceful in my mouth, much darker in meaning.

The human put their hands to their sides, making triangles with their arms. "It's impossible. But, I mean, look at you… You're a stone grotesque come to life."

Humans, with their frenzied, short lives, must not consider stone to be living. This was not correct; however, my voice felt raw from use, so I did not attempt correction.

"This is very fucking weird. How did it happen?"

"Do not know."

The human wrinkled their face skin, which I was beginning to understand signaled a question forming. "When did you learn language? How are you understanding me?"

"Watched. Listened."

"You just picked it up?"

I looked at my clawed hands.

"Oh, no, not—like, you just paid attention and you understood?"

"Stone has time."

The clock tower across the city chimed: one, two, three, four, five, six.

"Shit! Speaking of time. I need to get ready. I'm the mezzo lead."

"Met-so."

"In the opera. Čert a Káča. It's Dvořák. Tons of fun."

"Sounds? And light?"

They laughed. "Yeah. Lots of music. Lots of singing."

"Singing?"

The human inhaled a wind, and when they opened their mouth, let out such a sound, like sunbeams dancing gold upon distant water.

"A bit like that," they said.

I longed for them to sing again, longer, so that I could watch their body, see how flesh made this noise. But the human said they could not be late, "the show must go on, even when miracles are happening," by which they meant me, and so we went back. They left me in the dressing room, said "wait," said "we'll figure out what to do," said "maybe I'll have a brainwave while I'm singing." And left.

But how could I remain, knowing there was music? My body ached. I longed for relief, for the magic sounds of flesh.

I ventured out. All was empty. Remembering how I had been banished from the deep-dark, I contrived to find a different vantage point from which to see the pool of light where the humans gamboled.

Through wandering, trial and error, following the music, finally I opened a door into a huge, airy room blanketed in darkness. At one end, there was the lighted space, a shining rectangle. Only it looked different than when I had first seen it. Instead of the jolly humans and their dancing, here was a red and menacing space, with smoke pouring about, and bars of huge gates. Chains rattled. And the humans who rushed about—were they humans? They had horns, tails, and their skin was mottled. They looked…like me.

Were these my stone siblings, finally wakened? For a moment I had hope that I was no longer alone. But I quickly saw from their fluidity of movement, the speed and grace with which they ran, that their bodies did not pain them. These were humans, not grotesques. I could not understand. Why would humans make themselves look like grotesques to sing and dance?

Then, the human who had befriended me stepped into the lights. They joined their voice to the music. They played with sound as wind plays with leaves. First it whipped this way, then it curved, and spiraled, fast, then slow, rippling, then pouring. They sang in words I did not comprehend, but their actions were shockingly clear.

This human menaced and, yes, even struck, those ones made to look like me. Such fury! Such hatred and contempt!

Into the music came cacophonous, mocking laughter. For the black space around me was full of humans, seated, watching the events unfold. I'd had no notion they were there, but there were hundreds, if not thousands. And all were in agreement: this abuse of grotesque creatures was humorous. No one intervened. They laughed and laughed and laughed.

I was cold, as when standing in the rain. The human had spoken to me with friendliness. Instructed me to remain. Perhaps once they were finished here, they meant to bring me into the light and attack me in such a way. Humiliate and beat me. Expose my weaknesses. Maybe even kill me, in the way of flesh.

I scrambled backward, out of the darkness. As fast as I could with the pain in my joints, and the curving hindrance of my claws, I ran, seeking safety. Only one place to go: I fled to the roof. The plinth upon which I had spent hours and days and years, from which I had seen sunsets and moon rises and watched the stars spiral through their dances with the solid company of my siblings. The home I had abandoned.

I climbed onto my perch. Crouched. Curled my arms around my legs. Eventually, down on the street, miniature people streamed forth like ants. The opera must be over. The human would return to the dressing room and wonder what had happened. Perhaps they would come looking for me. I would not be taken in again. Though their music offered me temporary relief, there was no place for me among humans.

Nor did I belong here, among my siblings. For the longer I

was still upon the plinth that had been mine, the further gravity forced my joints apart. Muscles peeling up from their bones. Vertebrae compressing. Tailbone sagging. Resisting this dismemberment was constant struggle.

The human had said "miracle." Stone turning to flesh meant "miracle." Was it? How could suffering be miraculous? I had not asked for flesh. I had not asked to be a miracle. Nowhere in my stone body had been a desire for this excruciating, fast-paced sentience. This crushing solitude.

The space between the roof and the ground pulled. Urging. Easier, to give in. To follow gravity, before it could pull me apart, piece by piece. To fall. What would falling feel like? The birds knew. The larks let go of their perches and dove.

I balanced, feeling out my tipping point, the pressure of my weight crunching back and forth on the balls of my feet. Bones grinding against flesh, yearning to meet the stone. This fragile skin could not hold all of this pain forever. I balanced, balanced, my muscles resisting, but beginning to burn.

Fallon

David Corse

David Corse (he/him) is the pen name for David Cross, a dark fantasy author and movie podcaster from the Midwest. You can find his work in Split Scream Volume 6 *by Tenebrous Press and Gamut Magazine. When not writing, David co-hosts Award Wieners, a pun-filled podcast about Academy Award Best Picture winners. He is also a frequent guest on the Movie, Films & Flix podcast, where he chats about slashers, creature features, and ghosts. You can chat with him on Twitter @itsmedavidcross.*

***

The Death Bird lands on my fire escape, sorrow in her eyes. I've summoned her to take the shape of my deceased lover and soothe my grief.

"Your payment?" the Death Bird asks in a voice as gentle as morning dew.

"The day Fallon and I met," I reply, tears welling in my eyes at the thought of relinquishing the memory for the Death Bird's balm.

I tell the creature our story: how our friend, an amateur matchmaker, wrote obscene limericks for us to read at an open mic night, how Fallon's face was the color of ripe strawberries as she delivered her lines in a stuttering giggle, how I panicked and she told me to read them to her alone. I shared how I'd never seen a woman as beautiful as her, how her chestnut brown curls framed her playful face, and how the way she spoke reminded me of twinkling stars.

I told the Death Bird how my knees shook as we kissed under a street lamp, moths circling.

"A heavy price," the Death Bird says when I finish. "In the morning, this memory will be forgotten, and you will not recall summoning me. Is this truly the price you wish to pay?"

I consider the Death Bird's words and search my forlorn mind for alternative memories to barter, and then fall to my knees at my discovery.

There are no birthday celebrations or anniversary dinners. No concerts or movie nights. I cannot remember the first time we made love or when we moved in together. I have no memory of proposing or our wedding day. I am certain I gave her a pet name, but it is a clinical knowledge like an encyclopedia entry. I beg my tongue to remember the name's shape in my mouth, but it does not.

"This is the only memory I have left," I say, weeping freely. "How many times have I summoned you?"

"I cannot say," the Death Bird replies and drops on graceful black wings to the floor before me. "You have summoned me, and I have answered. What is your payment?"

"I'll give you other memories," I say, desperate to quiet my heart. "You can have my mother's face and my father's voice. My childhood home and the summers of my youth. All of these."

I squeeze my eyes shut and cover my face, ashamed of my weakness and terrified of my longing. How long will this go on until all I am is my last memory of Fallon?

"Do you accept my offer?" I ask the Death Bird.

"Yes," she says in Fallon's voice.

The Tales of RG Sley

Blessed

KC Grifant

KC Grifant is an award-winning writer based in Southern California who creates internationally published horror, fantasy, science fiction, and weird west stories. Many of her short stories have appeared in podcasts, magazines, games, and Stoker-nominated anthologies. Her weird western novel, Melinda West: Monster Gunslinger *(Brigids Gate Press, 2023), described as a blend of* Bonnie & Clyde *meet* The Witcher *and* Supernatural, *ranked #1 in Amazon New Releases for Western Horrors.* Melinda West and the Gremlin Queen, *releases in 2025. She is also the author of the short story collection* Shrouded Horror: Tales of the Uncanny *(Dragon's Roost Press, 2024).*

In addition to writing, she is the co-chair and founder of the Horror Writers Association San Diego chapter, a short story instructor, co-creator of Monster Gunslingers The Game, *and member of numerous writing organizations, including the Science Fiction and Fantasy Writers Association. Learn more at* www.KCGrifant.com *or @kcgrifant.*

ভয়

The bullets whizzed around Carla, sending up puffs of decimated corn stalks in the fields. She ran a hand over her enlarged belly.

"Get down!" A voice yelled from the stalks.

Carla ignored it and swayed instead, a little dance to soothe her unborn. Fate—a higher power—would protect her, as she believed all her life it would.

Even when everyone had said something was wrong with

her.

Even when everyone had said she hadn't prayed enough, hadn't *wanted* it enough. But she had wanted to carry life, more than anything. She had tried everything the commune members suggested, from sucking down putrid tea to letting the commune leader try and try again to create life in her.

Funny, Carla mused, that she hadn't been gifted with life until she was faced with so much death.

"Get down!" the voice screamed again.

Next to Carla, something dropped.

A head.

The head rolled a few feet away, severed, its hair neatly braided. Where the neck would've been was a trail of smoke instead. The weapons in the sky were effective, targeting people like mosquitos in a zapper.

Four people huffed and ran through the corn, louder than laboring cows.

"What's—No! *Miriam*," A bloodstained, petite woman screamed when she spotted the head.

"We can't stay," a tall woman said. Her intense gaze shot up overheard. "They're here."

The two men with them nodded urgently.

Carla closed her eyes. She was protected by holiness—she didn't need to run.

"Hey. Listen." The tall woman grabbed Carla's hands. "I'm Angelica. The invasion is here, now. We're losing. We have to get out of their line of sight before we end up like…"

"Don't bother," one of the men said. "She's in shock. She'll just slow us down. Knocked up too."

"No, we protect our own," Angelica said, and the words rang familiar. It was like what Carla's commune leader would say when he was still alive. It felt like a lifetime ago that Carla had heard his daily speeches, even though it had been just a few days since the invasion. Since the commune had caught on fire.

A passing asteroid, the Internet and news sources had claimed when the strange fires started. Turned out to be some-thing else. Some*things* that evaded sight, radar, detection while reigning down fire and noise from the sky, harnessing lightning itself to split people in two. Carla had witnessed it with her own eyes. Their commune leader had beseeched the other-worldly visitors from his wooden stage before a bolt cast his screaming figure into blue and purple flames.

While the other commune members ran in a panic, an over-whelming awe hit her, along with a relief so great she clumsily sank to her knees. Never again would she need to see the lead-er's fingernails, always immaculate and long, raking over her bare shoulders. Never again would she have to feel the dread blanket her as she faced his door.

The Internet called them *invaders*.

"The invaders are on us," one of the men said now and grabbed Carla's arm. He dragged her through the corn field. "We can take cover in the barn."

"If we can get out of their line of sight, we might make it!" Angelica said while they ran.

Carla cradled her stomach and half-jogged, best she could, with the others. They didn't understand what it was to be an expectant mother. She wasn't that mobile, invasion or not.

The bloodstained woman moved ahead of them, occasion-ally shooting out a spray of bullets upwards when shadows moved overhead through the clouds. The bullets were too loud, far too loud, but got lost in the hum of the ship over-head.

The humming had started along with the invasion, a sound

like motors whirling above them. At first it had reminded Carla of a giant cicada. Now, she didn't mind the sound anymore. The invaders, whatever they were, had freed her from the commune, freed her to raise her baby as she wished.

They made it to the barn on the edge of the commune and barricaded the door before introductions. The ones named Omar and Kil investigated the corners for gaps. It almost made Carla laugh. Surely the invaders could easily get in if they wanted. Omar pulled out a little electronic device. A radio with a cassette player, Carla recognized. Her dad had had one in a box of his old stuff.

"The invaders don't like certain sounds," Angelica explained. "Recorded music acts as a barrier. Weird, I know, but it's something. Can you tell me about this area? Any food, weapons?"

"There's no food," Carla said at last. "It all burned in one of the falling stars."

"How did you survive?"

"Blessed," she said. "Blessed to carry life, blessed to survive."

A beat of silence from the others, the cassette player wailing pop music, forbidden in the commune. The invaders' droning sound had receded.

"God, these religious types," the bloodstained woman, Talee, said, and shot Carla a look like she was week-old meat. Carla wouldn't let it bother her. Just because they didn't give themselves over to a higher cause, others thought they were better. Smarter.

"Faith is about total belief. If you do that, nothing else matters," Carla tried to explain.

"Nothing really matters if we're the last of mankind," Kil said. He hadn't stopped trembling since they got to the barn.

"Humankind," Omar corrected. He had a glazed look like some of the commune members when the invaders first arrived. Shock, Carla supposed.

"What do you think they want?" Kil said.

"Who knows," Talee said. "Water? The planet for themselves?"

"Maybe they'll see how bad we screwed it up and change their minds."

"You hear how some people are changing? Like *metamorphosizing*…"

Carla tuned out the conversation, perching on a pile of rotting wood and rubbing her uterus in the unconscious motion that had become habit.

"How far along are you?" Angelica crouched next to her with a sad smile.

"Just a few days."

"A few…" Angelica looked at Carla's belly and took a step back, uncertainty stitched across her brow.

"I told you I was blessed," Carla said.

"Heads up!" Kil yelled. Outside, the droning intensified to a chainsaw-like pitch.

"They protect their own," Carla explained over the noise. The day the reports came in about the asteroid was when Carla prayed harder than she ever had before. When the commune leader had fallen asleep, she had snuck a look at his computer to read frantic internet forum musings about aliens taking people for experiments.

"You can take me," she had said out her open window that night. *"If you let me have my own baby."*

"My own" was an important part of her wish. The commune took most of the newborns to the older women for childrearing. Her plan had always been to leave as soon as she was preg-

nant. To raise the child as her own.

The next morning, Carla had woken up to all the signs of pregnancy: her stomach ballooned up, tiny kicking like twitches from her belly. The invaders had heard her prayers. Accepted her and whoever else might have offered themselves up as vessels.

A true commune, she had thought that morning, praying in tearful joy.

"Carla! Come here!" Angelica motioned frantically from where she and the others crouched behind a pile of hay on the other side of the barn. Instead, Carla rubbed her belly while she headed toward the door.

To the cassette-player.

"Don't touch it!" Omar hollered and started running toward her.

"They need to come in," Carla said. She sensed it just as she sensed the life within her, waiting. It was time to—what did they call that maternal instinct—*nest*. The invaders needed to get everything ready for the next stage of their takeover, just as she needed to prepare for her child's birth. Her soon-to-be mother's intuition told her there were others like her across the globe, select humans that had given their bodies to usher in a new world. A world with the invaders as their fathers, midwives, mentors. Carla shivered in excitement at the thought.

She leaned down for the device. The invaders moved behind the barn door, starbursts of light breaking in through the cracks in the wood.

Ready for her.

Omar nearly reached her before she pressed the stop button. The doors flew open and dazzling lights in a color she couldn't define shot out, muting the others' screams.

The invaders floated into the barn, too bright to look at

directly. They loomed wider and taller than humans, ringed by prismatic flashes that pulsed in hums in a language not yet known to her.

Like they're made of star beams, Carla thought dreamily. One creature reached to her with the semblance of a hand. The finger-like appendages burned gently when she clasped them.

Their cool fire swept the other humans, leaving her unharmed. The baby turned inside her, eager.

She had known all along.

She was truly blessed.

Slick

J. Brian Reed

J. Brian Reed built his career in advertising and marketing, so he is no stranger to tall tales, fabrications, and things that are just plain wrong. He holds degrees in English and Philosophy from the University of Southern Mississippi. He currently lives in central Pennsylvania. His work has appeared in Gamut Magazine, Hobb's End Press' Black Sheep: Unique Tales of Terror and Wonder, Crystal Lake Publishing's Shallow Waters anthology series, The Rumen Literary Journal, and Yabblins. He writes what he knows, which isn't much, so he fibs on the rest. You can hardly find him in the real world because he claims that hiding creates a wonderful mystique, but he does show up on X (Twitter) occasionally: @jbrianreed.

*S*chluumping…not a real word, but the best word to describe my mutated husband coming down the basement stairs to kill me, or whatever the things like him are trying to do to the people like me. I'm just about ready to give up for good, but still holding on, for a while. For a while.

I can't see him, but I'm trying. My fingers too slick, I can't hold the match, so I've wedged it between my teeth, and I'm attempting to strike it on the cinderblock wall behind me. Until then, my husband is there in sound only. I imagine his sleek form undulating stair to stair, gravity pulling the mass of gray and green farther into the darkness. My darkness. His squid-like fingers fondle the walls around him. His breath wheezes through what sounds like a curdled slime.

Was it the sound? The drone? The monk-like bass tone coming over the mountains that started about two weeks ago? I remember sitting with Margaret on the loading dock behind our store, the big-box store where we worked. It was nice to sit and watch the sun fall on the backdrop in the days right before winter always set in. That night we watched the fires on the mountainside. And the smoke, white garland on a dying Christmas tree. And we wondered why. What are they burning up there? Why are they burning it? Is it causing that noise, the hum? Listen long enough and it goes deep in your bones, a shivering in the marrow. Makes you sweat. At least that's what we thought it was.

But it wasn't sweat.

This sound, subtle but unsettling, this *basso profondo* from the horizon keyed in on a trigger inside of us all, some more than others, some faster, some slower. It seems like the homeless found it first as they were the first to be discovered, dead or molting, oozing into the final stages.

That's when I first heard the *schluumping*. On the dock with Margaret. Birds flying on the smoke gray sky. The last delivery truck for the day wheeling past the dumpsters. Quiet enough now to hear it. And the moans. And the wheezing. Not my husband, this one. Not yet. This is still early on with everything. Margaret and I saw two glossy hands trying to grab… failing to grab…anything, from the inside of a metal garbage can. He was stuck in there, we figured. But how? How do you get stuck in a garbage can? Why can't you just stand up? And we approached cautiously. Margaret suggested we get Ron, the manager. I kept on approaching, one hand in front of me, for whatever good that would do, seemed right at the time. And there he was, the homeless guy, slick and shining with the stuff, the oil that made him too slippery to stand, to bolster himself on the can, on anything, so he could get out of there. He grabbed for my outstretched hand. I pulled back. The momentum tipped the can and he slid onto the pavement. Half of him did. From the waist up he was decidedly still human. The rest, the waist down, was an indecipherable mess, a slough of worm-slime and organic filigree, writhing with a mind of its own.

A frazzled, damp cigarette dangled from his slimy lips. "I need a light," he said.

We called 911. Paramedics could barely collect the slimy mess in a single heap on the stretcher. He slopped off three times, if not four. Never got his last cigarette. The write-up in the paper said he had completely dissolved into a foamy residue they were still trying to remove from the emergency room floor.

And on it went. Apocryphal stories circulated in whispers, from restaurant bars to sitting rooms to church hallways.

A mother, frustrated from unsuccessfully trying to breast-feed her child, was found dead in her bathtub. Her skin was too slick. It was on the baby too, his little lips too slick. He couldn't latch. She could barely hold on to him. And the numbness that came with it, hard to know what she was touching and not touching. The oil was thin, like a balm, and it came from her own pores as any body oil might naturally do. Yet it was different. It clung like cooking spray to the skin from which it came. But it clung to nothing else. Nothing else at all. She could barely turn the knobs to start the bath water running. It must come off, she thought. With water. With soap. Shampoo. Something. And the tub, it filled, with her in it, and the baby too, ten weeks old. Bathing was impossible. Staying upright was impossible, especially on the wet, white porcelain. Exhausted from the struggle, they slowly sunk below the water line. An aunt, coming home from work three hours later, found them. The phantom slickness caught the overhead light making swirling rainbows on top of the water.

An elderly mortician, Andrei Munteanu, was reminded of superstitions from the old country when bodies arrived from the morgue already exsanguinated. Bloodless, yes, but not empty. Full and soaked they were, with a clear, viscous substance; he watched it swirl and congeal, finally clogging the pipes and the drain of his preparation tables. Over the lip and onto the floor, it tended to move when he looked away. Approaching carefully, suspiciously, again trying not to indulge the haunt-frightened upbringing of his black mountain origins, he went on hands and knees to inspect it more closely. One fingertip. He touched it, the gel, the slime. Within the space of five minutes, he watched his fingernail melt away, then the skin and the bone beneath. Having decided it wasn't going to stop, not happy at all with just the taking of such a small amount of flesh, he amputated the carnivorous slickness from the rest of his hand. And then he cut off his entire left hand. Then at the elbow right before he called the police to come rescue him from a mess that had already dissolved the tips of his shoes and at least three toes while he was concentrating so diligently on the rest of his rotting arm.

And it wasn't just people, but animals and trees, living things like bugs, birds, and the grass on the lawns. Like morning dew, the slick oozed to the green grass tips and a pack of

neighborhood dogs found themselves slopping around in the
mess. No leg would stand, they writhed on their backs and
bellies, snapping at nothing, angry nonetheless at this invisible
perpetrator that kept them from their early morning rounds.
A neighbor watched from a window, unable to help, knowing that setting one foot on the oozing front lawn would put
her in the same jeopardy, an even worse jeopardy than the
one that made her unable to hold on to her own toothbrush
or coffee mug that morning. Her slippers would not stay on
her oily feet. Her robe would not stay on her slick-smeared
shoulders. Naked, she struggled to cross the hardwood floor
between her living room and her bedroom. And that mountain
noise, the murmuring horn sound, vibrated through the walls
of her four-bedroom ranch-style suburban home. Enough to
start anyone off to a bad day. Enough to drive anyone to the
tilt-minded murder of a sister whom she now claimed to never
really like at all. And for a sister to sprout gills and pterodac-
tyl wings seemingly overnight was an abomination that must
be dealt with in the quickest of ways. She had stabbed and
stabbed until the knife handle slipped loose from her slimy,
wet fingers.

The stories proliferated, across news and social media, the
details getting warped and skewed along the way. A bus driver
took himself and the bus at full capacity, at full speed, through
a downtown store front window. A bride had a meltdown,
literally, before God and everyone at the altar just before the
ring slipped off her slick finger. Her ring tinked on the marble
underneath the front pew. No less than eighteen young skat-
ers came away, bones broken, from the skatepark when their
fingers could no longer grasp the skateboards beneath them.
The basic story remained the same. It would be funny if the
endings weren't so horrible. Everything was oozing. And the

smoke-soaked mountains kept droning. No one knew where it was going. No one knew why they reacted the way they reacted.

It's raining again now. Not really rain, but the best way to describe the oil, the grease, the *smegma from outer space*, now falling from the clouds to cover all the inorganic things unable to produce the substance through their own pores. We're dealing with an intelligence far beyond our own. I can hear it snicking on the rocks in the bottom of the basement window wells, coming down in dollops at times. My husband is off the stairs now. The schluumping is now a slurping and a sucking, modified appendages to enhance motility across the painted cement floor. Still slick, he makes slow progress. His smell drifts closer, pungent and unpleasant, an uncleaned reptile cage sort of smell. I'm working still at striking this little match between my teeth, trying hard not to let my greasy lips touch the wood. To lose the match at this point would be a disaster. It's all I have left. The only key out of this.

I remember when it all came to me clearly.

Margaret and I, back on the loading dock the day after the trash can incident. Manager Ron had the stockroom crew poking around in the dumpsters with broom sticks. The smoke from the mountains fed the clouds overhead. Black winged silhouettes roiled in the mist, seeding the atmosphere for the slick rain nobody was expecting. The drone wailed on. All townspeople had heads down, talking, following the stories, wondering which neighbor was going to turn up next as a sloppy, slurpy mess.

Margaret: "I wonder why he wanted that cigarette so badly?"

Me: "He didn't want a cigarette. He wanted a light."

I didn't know exactly how all the pieces connected in my

head. And I didn't know exactly how I was so completely convinced I was right. But it worked, for me, at the time.

The homeless man wanted a light. He wanted the fire. Because somehow, someway, this muck slipping out of his pores reminded him of oil, common household lubricant. And on the side of that can goes a big red warning with exclamation points and capital letters. Highly flammable, it reads. Keep away from flame. And he knew. And I knew. This stuff was incendiary. It would go up in a poof with the slightest spark or flame. And whoever was left up on those mountains was fighting back, hence the smoke.

"Now ya see," Margaret said. "You are way too smart to be working at this dinky little retail job."

She was right. In a way. But I had chosen retail. The simple life. A job, not a career, because my husband and I wanted to keep our lives uncluttered, our heads clear. He had his side thing going as a sous chef for a local fine dining venture, and I clocked out every day and didn't spend one second thinking about the place until I clocked back in the next morning. I had college degrees, four of them to be exact, foreign languages and Francophile studies for whatever good that did me. I spent two years in Italy teaching English to wiry kids with tight pants and an aversion to pop culture. I saw places. I saw things. I saw people being people and realized that life is the same no matter where you go. Love the one you're with. Love the place where your feet fall, even if your feet slip and slide all over the ground when you land. With my husband, Chris, we made the most of it. And we loved hard. In a story like this, one might expect a snake in the grass, a bad apple in the barrel, but no. He came home to me. And we made love. A lot.

Tonight was the best, by far, to a point. He came in on fire. I was ready too, just a bathrobe and my hair done up the way it always reminded him of our honeymoon spent in the islands. He was slippery with the stuff, just enough to be sensual like the hot/cool intimacy topicals they hide in the back of the beauty department. It worked its magic, for a while.

We went at it like rabbits. Moans and panting. Diving in deep, coming up occasionally for a sharp gasp of air. I licked down his slick abdomen and the softer parts below. He found nooks on my body I didn't know I had, and they exploded in nerve-blasting ecstasy, for a while.

Then, without shape, notice, or definition, a line was crossed. The feeling started melting. The grinding, just grinding. I was on my stomach. He was on my back. He nipped, tiny teeth tips, at my neck and shoulders. It felt like love pecks. I soon realized he was drawing blood. Thin, pink freshets speckled the pillow by my cheeks. I was lost. In it. I cared only peripherally about what was really going on. The safe, sensible, smart me stood screaming at the foot of the bed. An atrocity was occurring. The lost me, crushed beneath the pounding thrusts of the man I'd swore to love forever, writhed and spread for him to go deeper. I felt it go in me, whatever it was. It wriggled and squirmed up into my abdomen, seating in a cozy fetal coil somewhere behind my belly button.

Spent, my husband, or what was left of him, could no longer maintain a grip on me, the sheets, or even the bed. He slipped off onto the floor, in a raging seizure, as the pieces and parts of his torso and limbs popped, cracked, and quivered, transforming to match a blueprint unseen to human eyes before. He rolled under the bed, and I stayed on top, listening to the violence of his joints and bones breaking then resetting themselves. I could feel metabolic humidity seeping up on the bedsides. I could smell that pungent stench, like over-sunned lizards.

Silence then. Long silence. Too long. That was when I heard the first rain coming down on the roof, pattering at the windows, ordinarily the kind of night for a hot bath and a good book. The ceiling fan spun in slow-motion circles. An antique alarm clock on the bedside table ticked with a muted chopstick tock. Sirens blasted above the dull mountain monk drone on the other side of town.

An unjointed, long, limp-fingered hand slapped over the end of the bed. I jerked my feet and knees up to my chest. The oozing oil on my skin made it hard to hold myself together in the panicking tightness my reflexes desired. Despite that, I did my best to recoil and stay ready to do what I had to do for whatever should come next. His other hand flipped up, bloodier than the other. The results of its work were obvious; two unseated eyeballs hung lazily on long red-purple strings. They were dead and unplugged. They saw me, nonetheless. I'd like to think that was the last time my real husband saw me. My loving husband, Chris, before his soul blinked out and joined the slipstream of the great hereafter. What remained wasn't him.

It's the only way I can justify sending this mutated monstrosity inhabiting his corpse up in flames.

And with that thought, I tilt my head just right, slide the match head just right, and the little flame roars to life, throwing a soft, circular glow on the basement floor in front of me. He's not there. No Chris. No monster. Not yet. The moving, the undulating of a hungry, evil something schluumps quietly in the darkness just beyond. I turn my eyes crossways to the match tip under my nose as it works its way down the match stem. Oh, dear God, we're on a timeline here. If this thing snuffs out. If this thing snuffs out…

I'm moving to meet him halfway. I understand the difficulty this creature is having with motion on slick surfaces. I can barely keep my bare feet and knees underneath me. I'm sliding on elbows and forearms, struggling to keep my head up, neck straight, and the burning match out in front of me.

It doesn't help that my first instinct when I jumped off the bed and started to run was to bolt out the front door on a lawn drenched in not rain, but even more of the vile stuff as it fell from the sky. And the difficulty I had standing upright by the furnace in the basement when I got here should have foreshadowed the difficulty I would have not just finding and holding the match box, but the trouble to come with securing one little match from a slip-scattered mess of them spread to oblivion across the dark basement floor. And this, not to even mention the twists and contortions I undertook to secure it tightly between top and bottom teeth when my slime-slicked fingers couldn't hold it fast enough to create a flame-inducing friction on the rough wall behind me.

I'm a mess. I am tired. I drip with the stuff and moving forward seems futile. I writhe and wriggle, on and on, feels like barely inches at a time. Centimeters. Millimeters. The flame shortens and grows bluer at the base. It disappears. My sinuses scrunch at the smoke. Gone out, for a while.

Limber, wet limbs curl around my arms and throat, lifting me up, face to face with the eyeless corpse head of my dead husband. I see it now. I see it clearly. The light. The flame. When it reached my damp lips and my shiny wet nose, it had smoldered a second before jumping to the lower half of my face. I, absentmindedly, forgot that I was incendiary too. My whole head, slick hair and all, goes *en fuego,* the flames licking happily across my neck, shoulders, and breasts. I look into those eyes again, deep, dark, and soulless. I study the cheek-bones and chin of the only man I ever loved. The dimple on the chin. The curl in his lips. I think of the tiny, coiled creature in my gut. I joust my face forward to kiss him goodbye, sending us both up in the cleansing, pure fire, smoking combustion. We will probably catch the gas line in the pipes overhead. It might take the whole house and the lawn, trees, and shrubs. Then to the neighbors and their own slick situation and the ones beyond that. Beyond that. Beyond that.

When it finally burns out, we all might be gone. But it will be gone too. The slick. And the long, hollow droning will fade once again to the empty existence of vacant, deep space, for a while. For a while.

Mortification

Angela Sylvaine

Angela Sylvaine is a self-proclaimed cheerful goth who writes speculative fiction and poetry. Horror-comedy fans enjoy her novel, Frost Bite, *a '90s sci-fi horror comedy, and her retro '80s YA mall slasher novella,* Chopping Spree. *For sad girl horror, check out her debut short story collection,* The Dead Spot: Stories of Lost Girls. *Her short fiction and poetry have appeared in over fifty anthologies, magazines, and podcasts, including Southwest Review, Apex, and The NoSleep Podcast. She lives in the shadow of the Rocky Mountains with her sweetheart and three creepy cats. You can find her online* angelasylvaine.com.

ᘇᕽᘙ

I could not resist the exquisite steel-eyed girl
Her lips on my throat fanning fire between thighs
Delicious heat turned to stabbing pain
I was to be punished for my sinful lust

She left me crumpled there
My heart beating beneath my breast
My tears mixing with rain from above
The sky perhaps mourned my fall that night

Ravenous hunger whispered I must take from others
Blessed sun now raised blistering boils on my sinner's skin
Senses corrupted into those of vermin looking for prey
I must repent and pay a penance befitting my offense

Dearest mother pledged to help me
The temptation of her veins constant torture
I undertook a fast of bread and water, body and blood
This tainted vessel expunged the sacraments

Demon's teeth sprouted from my gums
Filed to nubs and regrown each time to razors
Extracted from my mouth to leave oozing sockets
Lamentation filled those long, suffering hours

All the while the lonely came, drawn by Satan's snare
Attracted by that same heinous pull that drew me to Her
Mouth sunken and toothless, fingertips lengthened with claws
Still they begged with earnest for my kiss

My demon's teeth slice face and body in flagellation
The Devil still tempts from my steel gaze
Dearest mother blinds my eyes with those same teeth
In the exquisite pain of mortification my soul rejoices

A Wound in the Shape of Me

Mario Aliberto III

Mario Aliberto III's stories appear in SmokeLong Quarterly, Fractured Lit, trampset, and others. His debut chapbook, All the Dead We Have Yet to Bury, is scheduled for publication with Chestnut Review early 2025. He lives in Tampa Bay with his wife and daughters, and yet the dog still runs the house. Twitter/X: @marioaliberto3

☙❧

Beneath a pale moon and sparse stars, the child uses a rusty garden spade to dig dead worms from the dirt. Two long, white ones. She kneels in the center of an herb garden behind a house in the suburbs of Tampa, enveloped by the fragrances of oregano, parsley, and basil. The Florida humidity sticks her dress to her skin, and her legs appreciate the cool touch of overturned soil.

"Blood worms," she says, though she doesn't know if that's their true name. She had buried the worms in the garden in case she wanted to play with them again. And she does. She's a lonely child. When she's at school, the kids in third grade call her Witch Eyes. They make the sign of the cross whenever she's near. The child blames their cruel taunts on the contrasting colors of her irises, one blue and one green. She decides if kids believe she's a witch, she'll be a witch, although her mother has warned her all witchcraft exacts a deadly price.

The side door to the house claps shut as her mother struggles cardboard boxes into the back of their beat-up minivan in the driveway. Six months living in Glen's house. The longest they've stayed in one place. The child likes Glen the best of all her temporary fathers.

Her mother calls out quietly into the night. "Caroline? Caroline?"

The child arranges the dead worms into wide-parted lips as if mid-scream. She stands, hunched, keeping below the screen of herbs. She peels back a scab on her knee until the crust cracks open like a soda can tab and blood pours forth. Crimson splotches drip into the wormy mouth and the worms glisten darkly.

"Demon, tell me my mother's future."

The dead worms begin to wriggle, and the mouth speaks with a voice rough as untilled soil. *You will abandon your mother. She will die alone calling your name.*

Next, the child places a slug in the dirt above the wormy mouth. She wipes the slug's mucus from her fingers onto her dress and removes a salt shaker from her pocket. She salts the slug relentlessly until it shrivels.

"Her present?"

The butt end of the slug crinkles. Once. Twice. *I can smell the secret of your birth rotting your mother from within.*

How many times have they moved because of their secrets? How many different names has her mother given her? How many warnings that the child's true father must never find them?

Earlier in the day, the child had wanted to pick ingredients from Glen's herb garden for Spaghetti Sunday, but Glen said he was too tired to make tomato sauce. The backyard isn't big, and the herbs are in a small square plot, but she loves the garden. Glen taught her how to care for and grow things. He isn't usually mean like today. She wants Spaghetti Sunday. Maybe someday she'll learn a spell to get people to do what she wants, like the spell her mother uses to enchant old men into inviting them into their homes. The child doesn't want to leave this house, this garden, special to her in ways she can't articulate, but in the end, she knows it's yet another home her mother will force her to abandon.

Moving in and out of the house, carrying box after box, her mother whisper-calls the child's current name in twos like questions without answers.

"Caroline? Caroline?"

Two beetles, shiny carapaces, one blue, one green, skitter about the garden. The child snatches them up and places them above the slug. She lifts the spade and brings the flat side smashing down atop the beetles to keep them still.

"Tell me my future."

I see blood.

Glen had shown the child videos of a rock star named David Bowie who has mismatching eyes like her. They'd dance to his music while the sauce bubbled. She thought Glen was different, but earlier when he said she didn't need to collect herbs from the garden, he reminded her of the temporary father who lived in his car but wouldn't let her play with the steering wheel. The temporary father who lived on a boat but wouldn't let her fish. The temporary father who lived in a trailer park and fixed engines, but never let her hold a wrench. None of their eyes ever matched hers. Sometimes, she pretends David

Bowie is her real father, and his songs are for her.

From the driveway, the click of her mother softly closing the minivan's trunk reaches her. The child presses oregano leaves to her nose, breathes in their fragrance. It's only an ingredient, and yet it's the whole pot of sauce. The smell of Spaghetti Sunday. She wishes she could stay in the herb garden forever.

The child aligns two dead snails with cracked shells to serve as ears.

"Tell me my past."

I hear your mother agreeing to pay a blood price for life to grow inside her where no life should exist.

The color of the demon's smashed beetle eyes match hers. Like David Bowie's. She'd like to tell Glen, but then she remembers how she sank the pointy end of the spade into Glen's soft belly in the kitchen when he refused to make sauce.

"Tell me a secret."

The wormy lips pucker and make a wet kissing sound.

With each sacrifice, you become more powerful. Your mother is jealous.

She spades the shallow grave she dug for Glen, revealing fingers pale and lifeless as the worms. If she can speak to a demon with dead bugs, what could she do with Glen's body? Too bad her mother never lets her keep her temporary fathers' corpses to play with.

The child feels the heft of the spade in her hand. "May I keep this?"

Of course, my dear, the demon whispers as the hushed footsteps of the child's mother draw closer, closer.

"Caroline? Caroline?"

Rent One, Get One FREE

Rachel Searcey

Rachel lives in the Florida panhandle with her husband, two children, and two cats (1 black, 1 torti). She's bi-racial—Indian and white— and grew up in Texas. She has recently ventured into prose after over two decades of producing indie horror films. Her work has been published in Cosmic Horror Monthly, Diet Milk Magazine, Flash Point SF, Aphotic Realm, Inner Worlds, and various anthologies. For more info about Rachel's films and published/forthcoming works, visit agirlandhergoldfish.com

❧

I wake with my face pressed into the cold ground and my head pounding. My mouth tastes like battery acid. I can barely make out anything in the murky, orange glow and my eyes strain against the darkness. Groaning, I rise to my knees and my head hits a low metal ceiling. I'm forced to crouch.

Memories from last night are hazy. I was walking home from campus and then—*nothing*. Was I kidnapped?

My hands find cold metal bars. A cage. Oh God. I yank on the bars, shaking them with all my strength. "Hello?" I call. My voice is thin, strangled by panic. "Please let me out. My boy-friend is expecting me."

Something shuffles against the ground nearby. Images from the true crime documentaries my mom is addicted to flash through my head. The bars tilt and warp. I shake my head until the dizzy sensation passes.

A slot, no bigger than my hand, opens in the back wall to reveal a metal plate and cup.

"Take it," a man says, his quiet voice startling me.

I hesitate but do as he says. The slot slides closed with a clang.

On the plate is a pile of purple mush, peppered with white flecks. Whatever's in the cup smells like cat urine. I hear slurp-ing and the clang of metal on the other side of the wall.

"Eat your food and they'll let you out."

A grinding noise, more shuffling, and a shadow falls across the cage door. I can't make out any details as the man's stand-ing too far away. He's a gaunt shadow against the dark. My kidnapper.

"Let me out of here!" I shout.

"Eat your food," he says before walking away.

"Wait, please don't leave me. Where am I? What do you want with me?" But he's out of sight.

I curl up on my side, my back to the noxious food. The day before runs through my mind. A stop at the pharmacy for Mom's meds. Chris called to ask me to pick up more wine for the dinner party in our new apartment. I had an afternoon shift at Publix before my evening class. Jodie was going to meet me after. The tears start when I realize I might not see my family or friends again.

The man bangs on the metal bars. "We have to work," he says. "Eat." He crouches down and all I can see is an orange glint in his black eyes.

Rank body odor rolls off him in waves, filling the small space. His hand snakes through the bars and he grabs my wrist. "Eat or we both get in trouble."

I wrestle my wrist out of his grip and pick up the plate, tasting it with the tip of my tongue while he watches. A shudder runs through me. I pinch some of the disgusting mass between my fingers and place it in my mouth. It sits on my tongue like rancid gelatin and I force myself to swallow. I cough and almost vomit it back onto the plate. I take the smallest sip of the liquid while holding my breath, but it burns my throat all the way down. Tears well in my eyes and my nose runs. I put the barely touched dishes back in the slot, which closes with a clang. The man moves away, apparently satisfied.

The bars slide down into the floor, as promised. I crawl forward until I'm free of the cage. When I stand up, my body tenses, ready to run or fight. I'm in a small room no bigger than a closet with no windows, just two cages set into a wall and a single door: the source of the orange glow.

The door opens into a larger space. I struggle to accept what I'm seeing. It looks like…a store? The front is frosted glass and obscures whatever is beyond.

The man stands next to a counter with a cash register, his gaze on the floor. I look around for something to bash him over the head with and make my escape, but there's nothing on hand. I keep my distance from him, worried he'll grab me again.

He's emaciated. Eyes glassy, shoulders hunched. A beard stretches almost to his waist and his hair is matted and filthy. He wears a wrinkled polo shirt and khaki pants with holes worn in the knees. His feet are bare. Bands of healed scars line his forearms.

I realize I'm wearing the same outfit but my clothes are new, and not the work uniform I was wearing before. On the left breast is an embroidered logo: camera with film reel and some text below, illegible in the dark.

The walls are papered with posters for films I've never heard of. The people have too many fingers. Their faces melt into Picasso-like distortion. Actors bear an eerie familiarity, like a mix of different celebrities. The text appears to be English, but the letters are assembled into nonsensical words and sentences. Hundreds of video cassettes line the gray display shelves.

The man stands, staring at nothing and smiling.

"Is this a prank? Am I going to be on TV? I could see Jodie signing me up for this." I look for cameras in the corners and spot one. For a moment, I'm relieved, though uneasy.

"Jodie, if you're watching, thanks a lot." I wave at the lens.

It blinks at me. A fleshy lid drops and then opens. What I thought was a camera is a black pod with a single, shining eye. I step back. The camera thing sways and then rises on a long stalk to get a better look at me. My breath catches in my throat and I freeze.

"What the hell is going on?" I ask the man.

"Act like it's not there." He walks over and stands beside me. "The customers will be here soon. Work starts when the doors open," he says, nodding towards the store front.

Shadowy figures pass by the doors, with a shuddering, unnatural movement. Inhuman. Monstrous.

I realize the man is shivering. His hands are spasming by his sides and his eye twitches. His face jerks into a grin, all teeth.

The doors hiss open. Fluting music trickles in. I think I recognize a hit from the eighties, but then it's gone, morphed into an ear-aching rhythm with tense percussion.

"We have to work," the man says, guiding me by my shoulders back to the counter. Everything is wrong. It isn't an elaborate prank. I've lost my mind.

I think about Mom, waiting for me with dinner back home. I was going to pay her a final rent check, tell her I would be moving in permanently with Chris, and invite her to the dinner party.

My rambling thoughts are interrupted by wet scraping noises, like a dog crunching on the bones of a boiled chicken leg. Tremors of fear run through my limbs. Synapses fire in my brain, telling me to *run*. My feet seem to step back of their own accord and I curl up behind the counter, halfway to crawling back into the cage. I close my eyes and wrap my arms around myself, breathing in and out like I learned in yoga.

"Welcome to Movies and More, how may I assist you?" the man says.

The customer's voice is a garbled, bastardized imitation of a human, speaking in broken American English. "Need new video film. My brood enjoy this." A cassette slaps on the counter and it slides off to land near my bare foot. The case is covered in a sticky brown goo. I make myself smaller.

"Yes, of course. We have many more films in the children's section. With your membership you get one free today."

The man leads the "customer" away from the register. I take a risk and peek over the counter and regret it. Beside the man is a hunched figure. What looks like human skin is stretched over a creature with the anatomy of a praying mantis. A tuft of black hair sprays from a too small head. The arms are short and the creature's appendages stick out, covered by flesh covered gloves. From the waist down, the suit hangs like a tunic, with the legs dangling to the floor. Bare feet drag along behind it. No clothes, but three purses are strung across its jutting shoulders. The thing chooses two videos and they return to the counter. Its grotesque anatomy gyrates beneath the human skin suit.

I can no longer fight the nausea. The abominable creature, the awful stench, and the realization that I'm trapped cause my stomach to rebel. I throw up the nasty food and water. It burns just as much coming up as it went down.

"Excuse me," the man says to the customer and then he's standing over me. "Get up. They can see you." He digs his hand into my elbow and I'm hauled to standing.

I wipe the vomit from my mouth and lean against the counter. My nostrils burn, scalded with bile. It's hard to breathe.

"I apologize for the inconvenience," he tells the creature.

The man presses some buttons and the register lights up, but the drawer doesn't open, no money is exchanged. He puts the videos in a formless sack and hands it over.

"Thanks to you," the creature garbles.

"My pleasure." He bows, formal and stiff before turning to me. "Smile when you serve the customers. It upsets them otherwise."

The creature shambles out of the store and joins the shadowy figures on the concourse. My feet move of their own accord and I'm rushing towards the open doors.

"Don't!" the man shouts, but I'm already through. Dozens of the deformed creatures cloaked in human skin suits turn to look at me. Orange tinted fog swirls, colored by an arched skylight spanning the entire length of the concourse.

A mall?

The creatures, laden with shopping bags, funnel in and out of endless stores. Lit signs glow in the orange haze. A mimic of "GAP" but the text blends into one another. "Express" written in childish squiggles with the wrong letters. The familiar red and white logo of Radio Shack, but rendered illegible and mushy.

My bare feet sink into the floor, some sort of quicksand the creatures have no trouble walking in. Viscous mud sucks at my legs. Living wires wrap around my calves and I'm pulled down, down, down. My hands scramble at the slippery surface but I'm swallowed up to my chest. The creatures gather around in a semicircle, watching me with their beady eyes.

"Help me, please!"

They paw at my face and hair with human skin gloves. A chittering sound crescendos, like laughter. The orange fog closes in and my throat burns when I inhale.

They ignore my screams. Bands of pain encircle my body and I fight the urge to surrender and let the quicksand swallow me.

The man hauls me out by my armpits and drags me back into the store. My skin feels like it's been flayed. He lays me on the floor and leaves me there. I catch my breath and get a look at myself. Painful red welts lace my skin, matching the scars on the man's forearms.

I curl into a ball, running my hands over my lower body which still aches and burns.

The man stands near the front of the store as if nothing happened. I struggle to my feet, legs shaky and uncertain, and grab him by the shoulder to turn around and look at me.

"Why didn't you tell me?" My voice croaks, damaged by whatever the orange fog outside did to my throat.

He shrugs. "I tried."

For the first time, I get a good look at him. His sallow face is marred by dark under-eye circles and strange gouges beneath an overgrown beard. Rancid breath pours from his mouth, lined with black and yellow teeth.

I back away, seeing myself in him if I stay here. My eyes dart around the small store, my brain grasping for a way to escape. There are only two rooms: the one with the cages and the main store, opening to the concourse. A large vent overhead pumps in turgid air. The sentient alien camera watches us from the upper corner, turning and winding to keep us in its sights.

I wave my hand at it and the giant eye follows the movement. A shiver of fear runs through my aching body. Nothing makes sense.

The air vent could be reached by standing on one of the display cases. There were no screws holding it closed. If I can get up there and try to pry it open…

Customers shamble into the store, a whole "family" by the looks of them. A dwarfish one amongst them appears to be a child. Its small gloved hand grasps the hanging human skin leg of its parent. Beady black eyes peer at me through holes in the mask, where the human eyes used to be. Moist clicking sounds emerge from the child's mouth, squirming beneath the taut skin. I move away when it raises its appendage, but it doesn't touch me. It grabs one of the boxes off a shelf and waves it at the parent.

Another family comes into the store and the man says, "Man the register, I'll deal with these customers." He doesn't wait for me to respond.

The parent thrusts the case at me. It's covered in brown sludge. I take the case between thumb and forefinger and walk over to the register. I push buttons until the lights and sounds trigger, like the guy did before. I hand over the case in a bag and bow.

"Thanks to you," the thing gurgles. Its sticky appendage

brushes against my hand. I wipe the brown stuff onto my pants but I can feel a lingering tacky residue between my fingers.

The family leaves but there are already more customers coming in. I don't have any more time to think because the rest of the day is spent at the register. I become numb to the grotesque anatomy and broken English. My hands are coated in slime. Some gets in my hair and hardens. I give up on staying clean. The welts on my arms blister and weep.

The creatures file in, returning videos and taking more with them. They disappear into the concourse, swallowed by the heavy fog.

I fear one of them will attack me and I'll be turned into one of the skin suits they're wearing, but they make no aggressive movements towards either of us.

When I ask about the bathroom, the man gestures to a hole in the floor near the cages. I wait until the store is empty to do my business. There's nowhere to wash up and no toilet paper.

I cry throughout the day. The man shushes me and tells me to dry my face off. "They can see you," he repeats like a mantra.

⚭

"I'm Alee, just so you know," I tell the man after the store closes.

"My name was Kevin," he says, eyes half-lidded and unfocused.

Was?

In the cage room, a panel slides open to reveal cleaning materials. Kevin hands me a chisel and a rag, for chipping away the dried slime on the counters and displays. Dried mud carried in from the concourse on the creatures' feet is swept into a small grate near the front. Together we straighten the video displays. My eyes cross when I look at the covers for too long and I learn to look off to the side.

All the while, the living camera tracks us back and forth. I can feel its gaze burning into the back of my skull. My throat is still sore and I dread going back into the cage to choke on what passes for food here. After dealing with customers all day, my voice is almost gone, but I have questions.

"How long have you been here?" I ask.

Kevin doesn't respond or even seem to understand what I'm saying.

"Did you have a family? Someone who would miss you…"

Kevin gathers the cleaning supplies and puts them away. The panel seals shut. When I run my hand over the wall, I can't feel a seam.

Kevin crawls into his cage. The panels in the back open, offering our evening meal. He eats with sucking, urgent sounds.

I'm startled by a rumble in the wall. A smooth metal door clangs shut between the cage room and the main store, locking us in.

I crawl into my cage. The bars slide shut and I'm trapped. Tomorrow I'll be released into a bigger cage to work and work and work.

I poke at the rancid food with my filthy hands, hoping it's different than what I ate this morning. But no, it's the same purple goop and ammonia-like liquid. I take a nibble of each and shove it back through the slot. I shout at whatever takes it away, but there's no response.

I pepper Kevin with questions. He tells me there were other "employees" but he can't remember how many or how long they were here. After a while, he stops responding. He's either asleep or ignoring me.

Hunger has me doubled over, curled around myself. I have

to eat tomorrow morning or I'll be too weak to continue.

There are no noises other than the occasional shuffle from Kevin. I can barely breath, between my scalded throat and nostrils. Even my ear canals ache. The hard floor digs into my back.

Whenever I drift off, I dream of the celebratory dinner party Chris and I were going to host in our new apartment. Then I'm jerked awake by the horrible sensation of drowning in quicksand.

I fixate on escaping, anything to keep my mind off the creatures and the store. My mind trips over the strange surroundings. The living camera, the human skin suits covering alien anatomy, the fake movies. Nothing makes sense. Are there other stores with humans trapped, like we are?

There's nothing to do except wait and plan.

ⱭℰⱰ

Five days pass. The offered food is the same, twice a day. What I call morning and night is about twelve hours in the cage and twelve in the store. We shit and pee in the hole. My body reeks like Kevin's, and my hands and clothes are covered in fluids: my own and the creatures', whenever they happen to touch me. The orange glow never darkens or fades. Our only signal the day is over is the dispersal of customers, the doors closing, and then the cleaning.

Every day I've been nudging one of the display cases closer and closer to the oxygen vent during cleaning when the store is darkest. Today, finally, the case is directly below the vent.

The doors close and my body tenses. I've been waiting for this moment. Kevin hands me the chisel and the rag. I start cleaning the shelves, moving towards the camera.

I throw the rag over the eye and dash across the room and scale the display case. It totters and threatens to tip, scattering

187

tapes, but I hold onto the grate. The chisel slides into the gap as planned. Working fast, I leverage the metal vent and to my relief it pops open on a hinge. It's just big enough for me to squeeze through if I can get up.

Kevin grabs my foot and I kick him in the jaw. There's a wet crunch and he crashes into a display, sending video cases flying. My legs swing wild for a moment before I pull myself inside. A pitch-black void opens before me.

The store doors open and an alarm sounds, a wailing cry like a distressed baby. I climb into the vent shaft, closing the grate behind me. I put the chisel in my pocket and scramble on hands and knees through the dark.

The alarm echoes, never ceasing. My jaw clenches until my teeth crack. I ignore the headache, slapping my cheeks to stay grounded.

I pass openings into other dark rooms, facsimiles of stores on Earth. Mannequins in the shape of those creatures, with human skin suits stretched across their frames. Another holds appliances like toasters and ovens, misshapen and distorted. Fake, like the video cassettes.

Exhaustion threatens to overtake me, but I keep crawling for what feels like miles. Store after store flashes past the grates and I stop looking. My vision spins and my breath comes in ragged gasps. I can no longer feel my hands or knees, banging against the metal. The still healing welts on my arms are rent open.

The air blowing through the vents picks up speed. I must be close to the fan. I can feel vibrations in my rib cage; a deep thumping from somewhere up ahead.

Hope and desperation spur me on and I clamber towards the sound. The vent shaft widens and curves to the right, ending in an immense fan. I fight against the powerful gale which threatens to push me back the way I came. The wind takes away my breath and for a moment I feel like I'm suffocating.

But I creep forward. On the other side there's some sort of machine room. With shaking hands, I use the chisel to pry off the fan frame. The whirring metal blades muffle any noise I make.

Cautious of my fingers, I jam the chisel into the outer edge, between the wall and the blades. There's a high-pitched whine and then the fan stops, jerking against the obstruction. I crawl between the blades just as the motor grinds and forces the chisel out. It ricochets around the vent shaft with a horrible clatter and it's lost on the other side.

The room is empty except for crates of merchandise and the fan motor. After fumbling around in the semi-dark, I find a door with a latch.

It's unlocked. I open the door a crack and am immediately blinded by daylight. My eyes adjust and I realize I'm in a lot behind the mall. I step out and the door closes behind me. None of those creatures are around. The ground is muddy, like the mall concourse. I stick close to the building where the ground seems to be paved. Towering vegetation, similar to pine trees on Earth, but with vibrant red trunks and blue needles, dot the landscape. Green light filters through heavy gray clouds. There's a rumble and a drop of moisture hits my cheek.

Rain.

I smile. I'm outside! More drops fall and I smell something burning. My face begins to itch and I scratch with dirty nails. Smears of blood coat my hands. Small boils rise on my arms and hands where the rain hits bare skin. Something slithers down my back and when I grab it, I pull away a chunk of hair, separated from my scalp by the poisonous rain.

I stifle a scream and run back to the building. The door is locked and I can't get back inside. Toxic orange fog builds in the low places first and creeps towards me. I must find another way inside.

From the outside, the mall looks like a large dome. There are no windows or doors. I edge towards one side, careful to keep my back against the wall. Small splatters hit my face and arms.

My bare feet start to burn. I realize I'm standing in a puddle of rainwater. Painful blisters rise along my soles and I can no longer suppress my anguish. My body gives out, unable to sustain itself on pure adrenaline. My cries are those of a dying animal.

The creatures find me curled into a ball, suffocating on the rising fog, covered in blisters. I feel their chitinous appendages lifting me. It hurts to move and I lay still, even though my brain is screaming at me to get away. They put a piece of fabric over my shuddering body and press a kind of plastic mask over my face and pure oxygen fills my lungs. I weep, thankful for the relief.

They carry me back into the mall. We pass shiny storefronts. I see human faces pressed against the glass. Tired eyes and wan faces like mine, like Kevin's.

A large centerpiece fountain holds a flickering holographic representation of Earth. A video plays: Human figures with lopsided faces and too many fingers laugh and cavort in a funhouse mirror of a shopping mall, eat mutated pretzels at the food court, try on clothes, gab with their friends.

An advertisement.

The creatures skate through the quicksand floor and I'm born back to Movies and More. They remove the mask and set me back into the cage. The bars slide into place. I lay there shivering.

"I tried to stop you," Kevin says.

I whimper, unable to answer, hating him. My teeth start to chatter.

"You're lucky they brought you back." He shifts around in his cage. "If you don't work tomorrow, they take you to the food court." His words hang heavy in the air.

The panel in the back of the cage opens and food slides out on the tray. Ignoring the pain arcing through my body, I eat my dinner.

Disciples of Broken Bones and Rotted Teeth

Michael Bettendorf

Michael Bettendorf (he/him) is a writer from the US Midwest. His short fiction has appeared/is forthcoming at Drabblecast, Sley House Press, and elsewhere. Michael's debut experimental novel/ gamebook "Trve Cvlt" out at Tenebrous Press. He works in a high school library in Lincoln, NE - a place he tries to convince the world is too strange to be a flyover state. Find him on Bluesky/ Twitter @ BeardedBetts and www.michaelbettendorfwrites.com.

Adam Mantle had that dream again where his teeth ground until they cracked and fell to pieces. Except this time, they didn't fall into his lap, but into the hands of Billy Bullard. Some of the fifth graders at Lincoln Elementary say Billy was a god. Half of his classmates would trade their crayon boxes with the sharpeners to be him. The other half would do anything if it meant he wouldn't exist anymore. They were the ones Billy seemed to love the most. The ones he would turn. The ones he'd attempt to coerce to join him in the society of broken bones and rotted teeth. They were the devout. The ones who'd be his closest disciples and spread the good word from the playground at Lincoln Elementary to

playgrounds and backyards beyond.

"I fucking hate him," Adam said, his gangly frame dangling from the monkey bars. "He thinks he's so cool. He thinks everybody loves him."

It wasn't the first time Billy showed up in Adam's dreams.

"He doesn't think so," John Nordhues said, swinging around Adam, two bars at a time. "He *knows*."

Adam's biceps burned. The skin on his palms pulsed as his weight worked with gravity to pull him downward. He clenched his teeth as his grip on the iron bars loosened. Dust dirtied his ratty, canvas sneakers as he dropped and hit the gravel below. His hands ached and smelled like his father's toolbox. Adam spit on his hands and rubbed them on his jeans.

"He's such an asshole," Adam said, grinding crooked teeth, as a stream of spittle clung to his chin.

John had turned around, still hanging onto the monkey bars, and tried to take them three at a time. "You only say that because the girls look at him."

Adam reddened, his embarrassment masked as anger, because nobody—not even his best friend John knew the truth. That he wasn't jealous because the girls looked at Billy Bullard, but because Billy Bullard didn't look at him.

"Fuck you," Adam said, and saw John's momentum get the better of him. His friend fell to the ground, slamming his right pinky finger into the gravel at an odd angle.

"Owww," John grunted, wrapping his hand in his dirty cotton shirt. "Shitshitshit."

Adam repeated, "It's fine, it's fine," without conviction. He'd turned to get the teacher on recess duty, but as he did— as if by divine intervention—he planted his face into the chest of Billy Bullard, who smiled with such charisma Adam nearly fainted.

"I'm sorry." Adam stuttered and tried to hide his uneven overbite, but smiled instead; betrayed by the involuntary tug of facial muscles.

"My oh, my. Would you look at those teeth," Billy said. "But first, let me tend to the wounded."

Adam held his breath as Billy Bullard knelt before his friend, cupping John's dislocated pinky between closed hands that Adam imagined were laced between his. Billy whispered into the mess of quickly bruising skin and bone while Adam watched suspicion replace the worry on John's face.

Billy rose, while John remained slumped on the ground, his pinky still unnaturally bent, for his finger was not healed by some miracle because it was not for him.

It was for Adam. This, he believed, because even though Billy held John's hand, Adam had heard Billy's promise clearly as if whispered into his ear: *I can't take the pain away. Not now. But I can make everything okay in the end as long as you trust me*—and Adam felt the warmth of Billy's breath on his ears.

"I already have many followers," Billy said. "But you two will be my first disciples because you witnessed. And you listened." He walked over to Adam, leaned in, and kissed his cheek. Adam swallowed hard as Billy turned to John and said, "And though you still doubt, one day you'll truly believe."

CR80

Whispers carried the miracles of Billy Bullard through the small Midwestern town of Bethel, down the slides and soaring through tire-swings.

"Did you hear?" children would ask through hay fever-coughs and ragweed-wheezes. *"Did you hear how he got them to quit serving ham sandwiches at Washington Elementary?"*

"And how the school is getting new playground equipment?"

"I heard he convinced the principal to give them all-day recess on Fridays."

Echoes of similar tall-tale spread like wildfire across Bethel, but Adam knew the rumors were simply gospel-gossip. Lies spread to make Billy Bullard out as some genie, giving children simple pleasures instead of life-giving freedom. Did they not see what he truly offered? The power over adults. Authority over parents. How could they be so blind?

Adam knew the truth.

Billy Bullard made parents see their kids, like when he convinced little Daisy Mendez to chew her nails jagged, and how Carl from the third grade finally got his parents' attention by picking at the moles on his arms, turning them into bloody constellations.

The three children sat below the wooden fort on the playground, their temple. The place Adam mused about his god's teachings. Where he learned about the parents who didn't love him. The ones who only told lies and looked at him like burdensome property.

"Did you quit brushing like we talked about?" Billy asked.

Adam's mouth was opened wide, his crooked vulture's bite on display for Billy to inspect. An indiscernible noise eked from Adam's throat.

"It's okay if you haven't fully. You'll get there," Billy said. "But it's important that you do."

Adam Mantle believed and proved his devotion one skipped brushing at a time—and his parents started to take notice—just like Billy said they would. Adam's mouth watered as Billy ran a fingernail down Adam's tongue, raking a scummy build-up of bacteria that'd soon be strong enough to make Adam's parents retch.

"They'll never put a vacation ahead of braces again, will

they?" Billy said.

Adam savored the saltiness of his god's flesh.

"Your bottom teeth overlap so perfectly," Billy said. "Never fix them. Your parents missed their chance. Don't give them the satisfaction."

Adam admired Billy's graying smile.

"And you," Billy said to John who sat, legs in a semi-circle, massaging his swollen pinky. "How is the finger?"

"It tingles," he said. Adam's scalp flared and itched, angry at John's deceit because he knew John's finger was fine. Adam carpooled with the Nordhues and rode with John to the emergency clinic. He waited with John's sister in the lobby. He saw John return with a splinted finger that he only took off at recess so Billy wouldn't see.

It was just like John to take that sort of privilege for granted; having an affliction which could be concealed so easily whereas Adam's was so blatant, so obvious. Every laugh, every class picture, every joyous moment betrayed by his crooked smile.

"That's a good thing," Billy said. "That's the privilege of good health leaving your body. It is a reminder to you—to your parents—not to take things for granted. Here, come. It's time for communion."

Adam sat eagerly awaiting the gifts from Billy. He dwelled on the promise that it represented and wondered when it would be fulfilled. When the pain would be taken away. Adam knew that his parents didn't care, just as Billy proclaimed, but Adam was impatient, too, with his god's delayed promises. When would he attain power over his parents?

Billy dug a plastic grocery bag from the gravel-covered ground.

"Take and eat," Billy said, offering Reese's cups to his disciples.

They sank their teeth into the cups and held them there, creating temporary impressions until the chocolate melted.

"Really sink your teeth into it," Billy said. "The cavities will grow in time, just as your faith has."

They washed it down with swigs of flat Coke from a two-liter bottle.

"What are you doing?" A small voice interrupted the ritual.

John hid his finger from his younger sister who peered at them through the wooden slats of their temple. He had a panicked look on his face while he dug around in his pockets.

"Where's your finger-pro-tec-tor?" June asked, stumbling over her words.

"Go away, June," John said.

"Looking for this?" Adam held out the splint, which John took and slid onto his finger. Adam saw John working on an excuse, scratching uncomfortably behind his ears like he always did when he was caught in a lie. Just like the times he said he couldn't sleep over at Adam's, but Adam knew he just didn't want to.

"Oh…thanks," John said. "It must have slipped off."

Adam had to be careful, because he and John knew too much about one another. Secrets could quickly become ammunition. Although June didn't notice the vitriol in Adam's voice, Billy did. Adam waited. For what, he wasn't sure. Some act of retribution. A scolding. A lesson. Something—anything—because a god that didn't act wasn't a god at all.

Chocolatey drool spilled over Adam's lip, ran down his chin, and dripped onto his shirt. And for the first time since it all began, he wondered why it never occurred to him to ask himself that question. *What are you doing?* Adam looked Billy in his mossy green eyes, trying to convey his concerns. What are *you* doing? What will you do? John's overt disobedience could not be allowed. He'd crossed a line, Adam thought. *Teach him a lesson.*

Billy sat calm, collected and returned Adam's gaze, sending a message. *Patience.*

"No need to be embarrassed, John. We're all a little forgetful sometimes," Billy said. "And she's only curious, as children are—as we all should be. Remember, we are to remain as children."

Billy stood.

"June, was it?" he asked. "Can you keep a secret?"

John had begun to speak, but was quieted by Adam, who now understood his god was plotting something more. "Are you ashamed of our god? Let us evangelize."

June nodded in response. Two spindly pigtails hung down the front of her shoulders like dirty-blonde clergy cords. For who could keep a secret better than a child who wanted to belong?

ᘒᘖ

Countless notes had been sent home to the Mantles, intercepted and thrown away by Adam before his parents could see them. Good deeds, in his mind. So how his parents found out was beyond him. Adam, not thinking about emails or voicemails, instead believed there to be a traitor among the disciples. He'd suspected John.

It was because of this that Adam found himself wading through parents during parent-teacher conferences. Adam sensed John's disbelief during recess and he was convinced his traitorous best friend was going to burn their church to the ground. Adam could not have that. His love and devotion knew no bounds. Adam could move mountains.

The gymnasium was full of overworked teachers and concerned parents. Adam sneaked between aluminum folding chairs and wedged himself underneath the refreshments table. He listened, but not a single parent mentioned their child's hygiene to one another—too embarrassed, Adam thought, to address their concerns. Selfish adults, only concerned with appearances.

And it was only after one of the school counselors mentioned words like *mandatory reporting* and *child protective services* to the Nordhues that John cracked. And Adam knew it was only a matter of time before their parents would talk to one another. Adam had to tell Billy—and his god would have to act.

It wasn't long before the temple was too small to seat the society of broken bones and rotted teeth. Billy's followers spanned the playgrounds of Bethel and his disciples were twelve strong. Among them, Adam Mantle with the silver-capped smile, John Nordhues and his splinted finger, and his baby sister, June, whose ears were rarely clean.

"We need to discuss this," Billy said, ripping the plastic bag of communion supplies.

"She's trying," John said.

"Then try harder," Billy said. "Your parents need to know they can't take you for granted. You are more than a tax write-off. You are more than a mouth to feed. You are a child to be loved."

"She's only six," John said. "Our parents clean her up all the time."

Adam glared at John through slitted eyes and said, "Try *harder*."

Billy shoved his hand in his pocket and closed his eyes, a performative gesture that Adam ate up.

"Perhaps we need to try something more drastic. Something that will require more than soap and water to fix," Billy said.

He pulled his hand from his pocket and opened it to reveal a red jawbreaker.

"Hold this in your mouth," he said. "We'll make sure they see."

June reached for it and Adam now saw Billy's plan come to light, but it was revealed in ugly hues; a reality his eyes couldn't comprehend. He understood that gods worked in mysterious ways, but this was different. The end hardly justified the means—right? Why should June pay for John's lack of faith? Wasn't the end goal gaining power over their parents through devotion, not acts of harm to one another?

John snatched the jawbreaker from Billy's hand before June could. Billy's nostrils flared from John's disobedience. Red dye no. 3 left a sticky stigmata on Billy's palm.

"Don't you see?" John said. "Our parents have always cared. Adam's too."

John popped the jawbreaker in his mouth.

"What are you going to do, you fucking freak?"

Billy only smiled at John's rebuke.

"Is this how I am to be treated? Have I not chosen you twelve? And yet one—no—more than one of you is the devil! And I love none of you."

At that moment, Adam saw Billy for what he was—an adult in child's skin—the very authority he was told to hate. He felt a pang in his chest, his faith gone by the sudden realization his god was false; his promise a lie. Adam heard himself cry out, "no," but it could not be heard over the awful crunch that resounded throughout the temple as Billy struck John in the mouth.

Moments later John spit broken pieces of molars and blood and the solitary jawbreaker to the ground. He wailed while the others scattered to find the teacher on recess duty.

Everyone left except for Adam, and for this, he could tell Billy was pleased. Billy gripped Adam's face in his hands and placed his fetid lips upon Adam's.

But Adam pulled away in defiance.

"Go away," Adam said. "I don't need you anymore."

"You've always been a bad liar," Billy said.

"Fuck you," Adam said, and pushed Billy away from him. Billy ran from the ruined temple toward the edge of the playground. The chain-link fence rattled. Adam turned his back on his god and saw his teachers and peers running toward them. There was a chorus of questions directed toward Adam. When he turned around to point where Billy had run, Billy Bullard had disappeared into the woods beyond the playground. Not a god, just a boy.

Apocalypse Francais

Michael Craigwell

Michael Craigwell is an American author who lives in Scotland. Originally from Kentucky, he has lived in cities across the U.S. and abroad, from Birmingham, Alabama to Chicago, Paris, Providence, Rhode Island and New York City. When he's not writing, you can find him walking his Great Dane puppy with his family in Edinburgh, where he owns a pub. He is represented by Lynnette Novak of the Seymour Literary Agency.

❧

Susan held my hand, asked, "Are you feeling better?" I nodded, watched the empty highway: tire tread, crows on a bloody furball. Behind the overgrown concrete sidewalls of the *Kennedy Expressway*, dump trucks and wrecking crews cleared the chock-a-block ruins of northwest Chicago housing towers, pummeling entire neighborhoods into red-dish-gray mountains of crushed mortar and brick. Through flicker-gaps in the highway wall, I glimpsed camouflaged troop transports and tanks and clumps of heavily armed soldiers. The last of the fires had gone out months ago, though according to the national radio broadcast playing in the front of the taxi-cab, there was still chaos as far west as Los Angeles, as close as Detroit. Unless the situation improved soon, the radio hinted that a second St. Louis—even a third —might not be far away.

She smoothed her skirt with my hand, then guided my fingers to her bare knee.

His last paintings were different, Van Gogh. The artist of color and swirl, of starry nights and purple-shadowed flowers must have known what was coming. Of course he did.

"New Jerusalem," the taxi driver said. "You must be happy."

On the back of his neck, a tattooed cross peeked above his shirt collar. He was a pony, probably born in some open-window tenement bed, far from the needles and blood machines. His dash console interrupted the national radio with staticky close-circuit cab driver conversations. I watched peeling billboards pass. A bare chested woman was licking a water bottle above the fraying words: *Drink Up.*

"We're very happy," Susan said. "Yes." She eased my fingers to her inner thigh, kept smiling at the driver.

"The Virgin bless and keep you," the driver said. "You are good people." He slowed as we neared a razor-wire military checkpoint. Above lumpy sandbags, a soldier swiveled a heavy gun, tracking us, and another raised his hand, called, "Stop the car."

We stopped fifteen meters from the checkpoint. Susan slid my hand up her skirt to finger her panties. I swallowed, felt myself blush, which only encouraged her. The taxi driver cranked his window down, offered the soldier a print-out of our destination and clearance.

When the soldier went to run a check, the taxi driver said,

"No problem, I ran another family to O'Hare on Saturday. They'll let us through."

Susan gave me a playful look and forced my fingers inside her underwear. "Great."

I yanked my arm away. "Stop."

"Jesus—"

"Just stop."

Embarrassed, she jerked her skirt to cover her legs. The driver frowned into the rearview, said, "There is a problem?"

"No," I said. "We're fine."

Susan glared at the soldiers. "You and your Goddamn paintings. They got there yesterday, don't worry."

It had been a bad morning and not just because I knew the world was going to end tonight. My collection was already on the east coast in New Jerusalem. I'd wanted to stare at Van Gogh's last works again, as if they would help me get out of bed. I couldn't stop thinking that the divorce, the end of civilization was my fault. "Your pills," Susan had shouted, "just take your Goddamn—" *"No."* Van Gogh finished his final works, *Undergrowth with Two Figures* and *Wheat Field with Crows* in the months and days before shooting himself in the chest on a Sunday afternoon in late July 1890. He'd fallen three times before hauling himself to Ravoux, the inn where he was living. He didn't tell anyone, just went to his room, and the next day, when Doctor Gachet said that he still hoped to save Van Gogh's life, Van Gogh replied, *"Then it has to be done again."*

The soldier returned our papers and rapped the top of the taxi. "Drive safe." We pulled through the checkpoint onto an expanse of blast-scorched cement. There were more craters, and finally, beyond mountains of residential debris, the hulking terminals of O'Hare International Airport appeared in the distance. We passed more soldiers and had to show our papers at a second, larger checkpoint to confirm that we weren't suicide bombers or militia or plutocrats convinced we could bribe our way to salvation.

"So now you're not going to talk, is that it?" Susan said.

The soldiers had lined up four monks at the edge of the highway and were binding their wrists behind their heads with plastic twisties. Somehow the monks had scaled the concrete wall and razorwire. A soldier kicked one of the monks, knocked away his poster. I squinted, couldn't make out the words.

"Jack?"

"Yes," I said. "What do you want me to say?"

Susan stroked my hand. "Do you still love me?"

All the reasons I'd left Margie had eroded. My sense of humor made Susan smile now, never laugh, and she had less patience for my melancholy. The discussions I'd once valued so highly were after-sex filler—anything sounds better when a pretty girl says it five minutes after ejaculation. Still, I was chosen, and it had as much to do with my parents' bank account as the *Bersunfan*. Everyone I knew had tailored brain chemistry, carefully plucked heart valves; we were the genetic elite, and we took it for granted.

"Of course I love you," I said. "Don't be dramatic."

But we would stop in Newark. That's as close as they let planes fly to New Jerusalem. Susan asked me again, and I apologized as we pulled through the checkpoint, glimpsed the monk's placard—*"What Is To Be Done?"*—and I thought about Van Gogh and about Newark and the end of the world. I thought about throwing Susan from the car.

⚬⚬⚬

"Let me hear you say 'uh'!"
"Uh!"

"Uh—baby, uh uh!"

"Uh uh!"

I finished my sixth *Jack Daniels* and shouted over the throbbing music, "You want me to punch you in the face or what?"

"You believe this guy?" Andy laughed, clapped one of his fraternity brothers on the shoulder, and the band sang, *"Uh! Oh yeah!"* "Jack had too much Jack."

The club stank of sweat, lilac perfume, and beer. My shirt was clingy, and I swayed with both hands on the edge of the bar for support. People wedged past to the roped-off dancefloor. Candy-electric light-beams dipped in the soupy air. The girl I'd come with, Rebecca, had vanished into the dancing press, and Andy—dumb, Harvard Law School, play-by-the-rules Andy—thought that was hilarious. I'd only been dating Rebecca for two weeks—to hell with her. I couldn't get the bartender's attention. "Hey!"

"How many have you had?" Andy said. "Five or six? Christ man, we haven't been here an hour."

"I *will* hit you." Why wouldn't the bartender look up? "Honey, another JD already!"

Andy pressed my credit card down. "You don't need another drink."

I shoved him, and when he pushed back, I slugged Andy in the jaw, and he tossed me to the floor to kick in my teeth. Numbed from the alcohol, I tried to stand and was jerked to my feet, dragged past the dancefloor and punted onto the quiet, Boston sidewalk. It was freezing.

In three months, I would graduate with a portfolio of worthless oils-on-canvas and zero recommendations. I would be unemployed, and with my Boston University scholarship-rent-money suddenly gone, I'd be homeless. Mom had dropped five-hundred grand on my prenatal therapies; lot of good that did. I might as well be an ordinary pony, with no warranty on my liver. I wasn't going back to Newark. Why the hell had I been so obstinate with Professor Martinez? "Artists have to eat," she'd said. "I'd prefer you not starve. If you enter the American Liberty contest, even if you don't win, it will open doors…" I'd called her a petty hack—God, I'd been so stupid. The mega military contractor American Liberty was reaching out to anyone who could draw propaganda posters. Those were good jobs, better than working a retail counter— *advertistas* got paid.

I felt a wet dog nose in my ear and rolled over.

A red-haired woman in a white lab coat stood over me. "I'm sorry," she said. "Calvin, no. Don't sniff him."

Calvin was a brownish lab-hound mix with thick jowls, and when I sat up, he knocked me down again.

She struggled with his leash. "Calvin, no! I am so sorry."

"It's all right—I didn't realize I smelled so good."

She helped me up, and—because I was still wobbly from the drinks—when Calvin jumped, he tackled me. This time, she laughed. "I'm sorry, I don't—"

"What's your name?"

She hesitated. "Margie."

"Are you hungry, Margie? My name is Jack. I'm hungry. I just got punched in the face, and I've been drinking on an empty stomach." Calvin licked my mouth, and I rumpled his ears. "Yes Calvin, I know you're hungry."

"All right," Margie said.

I looked up. "All right?"

She nodded seriously. "I'll eat with you." She noticed my swollen lip. "Did you say you were hit in the face? Did Calvin…"

"No, different dog—acting like a pony." I stood. "Do you

want me to walk him?"

Again, she hesitated. "No, that's all right." But when I insisted, she gave me the leash, and Calvin took us north. "He's really too big," Margie said. "I got him from the pound as a puppy. They didn't know he would get this big. Do you have something in mind for dinner?"

"Chinese?" We both smiled. There hadn't been a Chinese food restaurant in Boston in five years, since the Third World War ended.

I'd been sixteen the November before Armistice, and my mother had been waiting for me in the kitchen with a security envelope marked with a Selective Service, Washington, D.C. return address. Come February 9th, it informed me—the day after my seventeenth birthday—I was to report to the Army Recruitment Center on Clinton street in downtown Newark for a routine physical and uniform measurement.

"I won't go," I'd told my mother.

"Don't be so stupid all the time. Do you think you can trick these men? And what if you hide, huh? What then? No son of mine will hide while his relatives are sacrificing their lives. We made you better than that. What do you think will happen to the checks they send every month for your father, huh? Look at me, Jack. Do you think your drawings do anyone any good? I won't have you dishonor your father like this, not my son."

My father had been killed off the coast of the Babuyan Islands in the northern Philippines in the first months of the war. When the war ended in late January, just one week before my seventeenth birthday, my mother forgot our fight. But I didn't. Through fits of manic energy and soul-numbing depression, I attacked my canvases with brush and pen and knife. That long-ago rebellion was the reason I'd just been kicked in the face and would soon be unemployed. Still, I missed fried rice.

❦

"Why do you like Van Gogh so much?" Two months after our first dinner, and Margie still didn't understand? I followed her into the aluminum-lit lab where she'd left her car keys. "I know he's a great painter, I respect that, but there are so many others…"

"Painter schmainter," I said. "I like him because he was such a sexy man."

Margie laughed and swiped us into a lab of computer stations with transparent monitors. An empty white display dominated the rear wall.

"You've seen his self-portrait," I said. "Such *brooding* and *self-loathing*—he chopped off his ear and wrapped it in paper to give to a prostitute: What more do you want?"

Smiling, she searched the cluttered work areas. "I know I left them here…"

"You do nudes?" I asked.

"What?"

I pointed. "The display wall—what is that?"

"They call it a *Bersunfan*—a capsid catcher." When I didn't get it, she said, "It makes virus art."

"Virus art?"

Still looking for her keys, Margie said, "They used to do cells and bacteria—this one does viruses, which are less than bacteria, much smaller. Where the hell are my keys?"

"Do what—do what with viruses?"

She stared at the room, as if her keys might appear in plain sight. I spotted them under her chair but didn't say anything.

"We can measure the noises made by the components of cells, and now we can do viruses, which are a thousand times smaller than bacteria. Viruses are basically just DNA or RNA in a protein coat sack, like a teeny tiny beanbag."

"So you measure the *noise* virus DNA makes?"

"Yep. This translates the pitch into color."

"Why?"

"When you engineer a virus, the patterns are useful."

"They're under your chair."

She grabbed her keys. "You saw them the whole time, didn't you?"

"Can you show me the virus art?"

"You want me to turn it on?" She shook her head. "I shouldn't have called it art, you'll be disappointed..."

But I convinced her, and when the machines came on, the white board mottled with a slow yellow-blue haze, as if we were underwater, looking at the sun. My ribcage constricted involuntarily as I watched the yellow bleed to green then back in golden ripples. This is the sound of DNA.

"Have you listened to ours?" I asked.

"To human DNA?" She nodded. "They've played with *Bersunfans* in gene therapy."

"What are we looking at?"

"Influenza, a mild strain. That's the way the common cold sounds. I told you you wouldn't be impressed."

"I am." Just staring at this, remembering the textured Van Goghs I'd seen in New York...there was something else going on.

"Are you ready?" Margie asked.

I watched the blue-light swirls. "I don't think that's just color—there are patterns, see?"

"Jack..."

"That's language."

⟐

We were almost to Newark when I made a mistake.

"Why do they call it 'the garden state?'" Susan asked as we watched plots of factories and suburbs pass thousands of feet below her window. "Are there really gardens?"

"Yes, there are lots of local farmers—my father grew all his own produce."

"Your ex-wife lives there now," Susan said, stiffening. "Doesn't she? She moved into your old—"

"I don't know," I lied.

"You grew up in Newark, didn't you? It's where she went after everything." Susan studied me. "Why are you so tense—Christ." She snorted, looked back out the window. "Don't worry, we'll find you whiskey and a razorblade when we land."

"What?"

She smiled to herself. "Nothing."

We rode in silence. The tiny plane rattled and bounced. The loudspeaker crackled, "We're beginning our descent into Newark. Please return to your seats. Thank you."

There was only one other family—an elderly couple from St. Paul with a blonde little girl—on the flight. They might have been in their sixties or early nineties, it was impossible to tell. If that girl was theirs, she'd probably been created through injections and gene therapy, computers and chemistry; but, they'd won a life in New Jerusalem the old fashioned way, through chance. Not like us.

When we dropped from upper-atmosphere sunlight through a layer of murky clouds to touch-down on the puddled runway, Susan stood. "Well?" Military Humvees approached across the tarmac outside. "It's all right, it's just a stop," Susan said. "It's not the end of the world yet."

⋆

I palmed a foam basketball and leaned back in my chair. "Margie, the board is hooked up to the wrong station."

From her office across the hall, Margie called, "The intern's late—make him fix it."

The intern—perfect, just what I needed. Some Mumbai medical student with dreams of patenting his own retro-virus. I tossed the basketball, it soared into the plastic net taped below *Undergrowth with Two Figures*, a lonely painting of a couple amid wild yellow and white flowers in a leafless forest. The couple strolled between purple-blue tree trunks, the woman grayish and indistinct, the faceless man dressed entirely in black. Behind them, a wall of darkness hovered at the edge of the trees: completed sometime in June 1890, one month before the suicide.

"Nothing but net," I said. "You take the intern."

Margie stepped into the doorway. My office was three times the size of hers, with a dozen computer-equipment desks, crammed bookshelves, awards, a kitchen and full bar, and nine original Van Goghs.

"If the sequencer is screwy, you should have the intern correct it," Margie said. "Give him something to do."

"If I beat your time on the wall, you take the intern."

"Jack…"

"What? Come on, it's only fair."

I hustled her down the hall to the courtyard. Before transferring to Chicago, I'd demanded that American Liberty install a three-story outdoor climbing wall with a protective overhang to keep the brick and plastic handholds dry in the winter. When I made the demand, I'd never even been climbing; it had been a prick-test to see how badly they wanted my contract. I snapped a rope-belt under my white lab coat, found a handhold.

"What are we at?" I tested the rope, followed the line up to the top of the wall. "Forty-five?"

"I clocked forty last night," Margie said.

"All right, forty it is. Ready?"

"Go," she said.

I pulled up, found another handhold, planted my foot, and continued up. Arms straining, I passed the second floor court-yard windows. "Time?"

"Fifteen," Margie said.

Fifteen, good. I can beat forty. I climbed, heard the door slam.

"Time?" I shouted, still rising. I was eight meters from the roof. "Margie?" I looked down: She was talking with a tan girl in a tanktop and short skirt, only half-heartedly spotting me. I paused too long; I wasn't going to beat forty seconds now.

"Jack!" Margie shouted. "Come down and meet Susan!"

I did, and still panting, shook her hand. "Hi, Jack Vasquez."

"Susan is your new intern."

"Great."

I walked her back to my office. "That's the art-board. We call it art, but it's sound . . ."

"I know," Susan said.

She knows, I thought and gestured to the nearby work station. "I'm glad you're here. I have something for you to do already."

My framed diplomas and awards and paintings didn't seem to affect her. Plenty of interns—hell, even the boyish seventy-something CEO—bowed before entering. Susan smiled. "How can I help?"

"The board is linked to the wrong station." I indicated my electronic paintbrush and palette. "My wife doesn't talk down the viruses like I do."

"You like impressionists, huh?" she said.

My earpiece clicked. Margie was calling from the other end

of the building. I didn't have an implant, but I'd gotten into the routine—though I'd sworn I wouldn't—of never removing my plastic inner-ear insert so that I was always reachable. I only removed it to sleep. My right ear clicked again. If I wanted to answer, the call would automatically start.

"No," I said. "Just Van Gogh."

When she leaned over the workstation, her shirt slid up to expose a blue circle tattooed on her lower back. I answered the call. "Hi."

"Hi, I'm heading home," Margie said. "Are you going to be awhile?"

Susan switched on the paint-board, and a swirl of reds and purple flooded the screen. "Doctor Vasquez . . ."

"I told you, that's hooked up to the genome sequencer across the hall. I need you to fiddle with the router and link it to that machine there. Understand?"

"Is that the intern?" Margie asked.

"Yeah," I said. "I'll talk to you later."

"Do you want fish for dinner?"

"Sure."

"I love you."

"Love you too." I ended the call.

"Doctor Vasquez?"

I forced myself not to look at Susan's tan lines or the edge of her pink bra. "I'm not a doctor."

"But Yale—"

"That was an honorary degree," I said. "Doesn't count."

People always made that mistake. I hadn't gone to medical school, didn't even have a Master's Degree, and I never thought of myself any differently than I had before the 'Roeschstan Sequence'—I was an artist. Well, not *just* an artist. The Nobel committee had named it 'Roeschstan' after the German chemist—Margie's old supervisor—who had matched my paintings to microscopic fluctuations to mimic the noise of virus DNA. I'd had the idea that colors on a board might be virus speech, but how could that possibly be tested? Simple: I'd painted back. By routing the wallboard to nano-critter DNA, they'd created a hybrid virus, a virus-negotiator, to shake and shimmy in time with my colors. In half-steps, I—and our virus-negotiator—learned to speak, first with influenza, then with the honta virus, then with HIV. At first it had been guesswork. What does yellow mean? What does vibrant red signal? Gradually, I'd learned to read words in the electronic-ink. And I'd written back: *Don't do this. Don't transfer your DNA. You will kill your home, and then* you *will die.* The viruses listened. For lumps of genetic goo, they were surprisingly open to compromise. After all, the most successful parasites *aren't* lethal. It was win-win. While some scientists still insisted that viruses were not even technically alive, I negotiated with these microscopic beanbags.

After my discovery, there had been money and fame, and even more money when they realized that not just anyone could read the virus languages and paint back. Most of it was intuitive, which meant that I was in demand. And who had paid the most attention? American Liberty, a company intent on training super viruses to ignore future germ warfare negotiators: My job now, semi-top secret, was to poke and prod their engineered bugs until I was convinced that no rival negotiator could talk it down. In other words, they paid me ridiculous amounts of money to render my discovery obsolete so people would get sick again. Meanwhile, across the hall, humanitarian Margie was developing gene therapies to cure arthritis—but she never forgot who paid the bills. I was Mr. Big Time.

"Is that a protein coat emission…?" Susan asked.

"No," I said. "Of course not. I told you, it's hooked up to the genetic sequencer across the hall. That's human DNA, not a virus. It only looks similar—trust me, it isn't talking."

"But it…" she hesitated. "This is going to sound stupid. I'm embarrassed."

"What?"

She looked at her feet. "Will you take me to lunch?"

I fingered my wedding ring. "You're hungry?"

"If I tell you what I think this is, will you take me to lunch?"

"I know what 'this is': My wife is altering the human genome," I said. "Do you understand? Each of us has—eight percent of your DNA is composed of old viruses, viruses that stuck themselves into our ancestors like leeches in reverse, that's why it looks…" I hesitated. "What?"

"I understand," she said. "They sent me here because I can speak—I can read some viral color patterns. No one else in my class could, the viruses speak such a difficult language…" She touched my shoulder, and I felt heat between my legs. Stop it, she's—just stop it. "I think," she said, "I think it's a threat."

"It's not…"

But it was. I hadn't noticed it for the same reason Margie hadn't noticed the smear-glob patterns on her first wallboard three years ago. Susan was right. The green rings around the red pulsing interior indicated hostility. Anyone could see that. I let my vision blur to pick up the subtleties of the color patterns, to find words; it was the same technique I used to paint the microbial responses. The virus languages were all the same, really. I'd come to think of the differences as dialects, not alien tongues. These smears stuttered like a child. It was throwing a tantrum. That was silly. When I had it, I was sure I'd gotten the message wrong. My mouth went dry, and a breeze shivered the hairs on the back of my neck.

"Do you know what it says?" Susan asked, still holding onto me.

I said, "I'm not…"

Do what we ask or you are all going to die.

⁂

The champagne stung my sinuses, but I was enjoying the way the bedroom swam when I turned my head.

"Kids," I said. "I don't want to talk about that right now—Jesus, not now."

"Don't make excuses," Margie said. She sat crosslegged on the bed, her black dress riding high on her pale, flushed thighs, her cheeks bright from the wine, red hair curly and loose. Margie's neck and chest and arms—every bare inch was spotted with light freckles, and when I didn't answer, she leaned forward, and I couldn't stop staring at her breasts—that was good, right? A good thing to ache for your wife. So explain Susan.

"Jack, don't fall asleep."

"I'm awake."

"Just think about it then," she said. "It could be months after I stop taking the pills, and then another nine months before the baby is born—so even if I stop tonight—"

"Margie…"

"—it wouldn't be until *next* December. What?"

"You look beautiful."

She drank and held my hand. "Are you happy that I'm your wife?"

No, I thought. What is wrong with me? "Of course."

We kissed, and she said, "I feel like we haven't been talking as much, like you've been distracted."

"Work is just so—it's tough," I said. It had been four months, and I still hadn't told her—told anyone but Susan—

about my discovery. I still didn't believe it was possible. "If you get pregnant, and I'm always gone…"

Margie pulled away. "What were you doing when I called this morning? It went straight to voicemail."

"What?" An image of Susan on her knees behind my desk. "Nothing—what do you mean? My earlink was turned on."

"You have to answer," she said. "What if I need to reach you?"

"I can't, not when I'm working."

"Please," she said.

There was a strange desperation in her face. We weren't going to sleep tonight. It was going to be a bad one. The fights were wearing me out. She knows about Susan, I thought. No—how could she? "What's wrong?"

"What do you mean 'what's wrong'? You won't even discuss it."

"Children."

"*Yes.*"

I stood, steadied myself on the wall. "I'm not going to argue with you."

"You're just going to…it's our anniversary." Her voice cracked with tears. "I wore your favorite dress. Didn't you like dinner?"

"I don't want to argue about kids, I told you."

"Why—when will you want to talk about it then? I'll be thirty this year, and I wanted to be young when we start our family. Jack? Come here." She spread her legs, forced a smile. "I know how to keep you here."

But I couldn't make the room hold still. "No. I'm going to the office."

"Why?"

Because I'm exhausted and scared and drunk. "I don't

know, I think I drank too much."

"Stop." She followed me into the living room. Calvin looked up with his sad, hound eyes from his usual spot on the couch. "Jack." Margie started to cry. "Please, don't do this."

I left without answering.

Christ, the last thing I needed to think about was kids. Not now.

I stumbled the ten blocks to my office. No one knew. An ancient virus in my DNA, embedded in every cell of my body—of everyone's body—had threatened me. I'd spent weeks trying to convince myself that I was wrong, that the wallboard was linked to a different work station. It was a practical joke. Someone had rigged a console in a nearby building and was beaming in bogus swirls—except it wasn't and they weren't. It was real, and when I had tried to respond, the virus had repeated its message: *Do what we ask or you are all going to die.*

I painted a blue and silver *Why?*, but it had only responded with orangish black: *Shut up.*

Back in the office, I grabbed my paintbrush and electronic easel. My ear clicked. Margie. I ignored her. When I switched the board on, the same red threat oozed across the board.

I jabbed blue and silver, rimmed the pixel-pattern with green and orange and tapped the button to send it to Margie's genome-station. *What do you want?*

The same red blotches obscured my painting. *Do what we ask or you are all going to die.*

I painted a blue-green *What?*, then added a reddish silver line that jagged across the right-edge. I'd never used red, only rarely touched orange. When I'd moved into the office, I'd even explained to the techies that I wouldn't need a red palette color—I wasn't planning to get aggressive with the diseases— but they hadn't understood. My handheld could generate any color under the rainbow. I sent the message, *Tell me what you want or I will stop talking.*

The virus's red-threat coiled and flexed, popping with silver bubbles. *You will shut everything down.*

Van Gogh had been mad. He'd disfigured his face, committed suicide.

I painted a silver-gray question, *Shut down what?*

More silver bubbles congealed in the red, now bright yellow and gold bubbles, bursting to black. Was I reading this right? No. I repeated the question, and it answered identically. This couldn't be right. I shouldn't do this drunk.

I don't believe you, I painted.

It responded with red, *Do what we ask or you are all going to die.*

I wanted to tear down the board. To hell with this. It was ordering me to dismantle society, to scrap technology and start over. How could I do that? I asked for details, and in fine yellows and blacks and silvers, it told me its demands:

One thousand people will gather in a new city. They will dismantle all of society, they will destroy all of their knowledge and return to primitive life.

And I answered with orangish blue, *What if we don't?*

A strict series of red and black bubbles advanced across the board. Oh Jesus.

☙❧

What made Van Gogh paint? Not success—he'd sold only two paintings. What virus created his madness? He was channeling it, wasn't he? His crazy French blood was speaking through him, using his fingers. I wasn't a Goddamn puppet.

If you do not do as we ask, we will kill you. Ten million will die every month.

My legs were shaking. As the champagne buzz faded, dread hooked in my chest, making it hard to breathe. My ear clicked again, Susan this time.

"Hi," I said.

"I know I shouldn't call," she said. "Can you talk?"

"Yeah."

I drew an orange-ringed blue. I painted, *Why? Tell me why!*

"Jack? Are you okay?"

When it threatened me again, *Do as we ask…*I cut it off: *Tell me why right now!*

"No, I'm not okay."

The silver-gray-purple response: *You will change yourself. You will erase us.*

"Today is my wedding anniversary," I said. "And I'm in the office." And a part of my DNA is afraid that I will alter it into oblivion. It's probably right, I thought. My great-grandchildren—yes Margie, if I ever agree to have any—may not even be recognizable as the same species. The human race is on a fast-track to perfection, but our soul—an insect we caught in our prehistory—has other ideas.

"I had a great time this afternoon," Susan said. "I was just thinking about you…"

The genome-virus continued, *We will start now. We will not stop until your world is dismantled.*

It's a suicide bomb inside our skin. I understood Van Gogh more and more.

"Turn on your monitor," I said.

"What—why?"

"Just turn it on."

A pause, and Susan said, "Okay…do you want me to watch something in particular?"

It's nothing. I'm wrong. I stared at a painting of a yellow field below a blue-black sky. A cloud of carrion birds soared overhead. I'd heard it was about the crucifixion, Armageddon;

it was Van Gogh's last painting, *Wheat Fields with Crows*. It had cost me half a billion dollars.

"Okay, wait," Susan said. "Something happened…"

So that's why he cut off his ear. "What?"

Susan murmured, "Oh God."

My ear clicked. Margie.

"Yeah," I said. "Exactly."

☙❧

"I hear tanks in the street."

Susan was knitting, listening to church-Latin rap on the wall-monitor, squids of colors blotting and flexing onscreen with the music.

"You shouldn't stand by the window," she said.

It was late, almost 10:00. I had to get home. How many nights could I work late, how long until I told Margie?

Heavy engines and steel-gear treads passed outside. I heard a jumble of soldiers' voices. In the ten months since the air force had carpeted St. Louis in napalm, things had only gotten worse. The mass deaths hadn't stopped, and today was the 12th. Every month, the virus took ten million people from around the world. Randomly chosen—great-grandparents, infants, strong men and women who had never been sick—they all collapsed, their hearts stopped at exactly the same instant. There was no logic, no negotiation. The virus never spoke again. The screen swirled with meaningless white-gray static; the deaths continued. Its official name hardly mattered. People called it the S-Virus, the Soul. God had changed His mind. This was not a disease or plague, it was a culling. We were cattle on a meat-packing conveyor belt at the end of time.

What if I hadn't understood the language—what if my whiskey-frustration provoked this? In the first months, I was forced to confer with the terrified men and women who ran the world. "Is it man-made?" they asked. "How can we stop it?" It is us, I told them. Somehow, a part of our genes—a virus at the core of our DNA—has sensed that it might be modified into obsolescence, and it is striking first. Everywhere. At 11:55 central time, on the twelfth day of each month.

We have to build a city.

"What if it's one of us?" Margie had asked after my mother's death in the third month. "What if it's me tomorrow—or you? Those people in the projects, with their guns…"

"They're terrified," I'd said. "What do you expect people to do? *We're* lucky."

How could I talk about this, how could I think?

"*You're* the one the corporations ask," she'd said. "You know more than anyone about this."

"I don't know anything," I'd told her, though that wasn't true. We were self-evolving. Our soul wasn't ready to be erased.

"It's impossible," I told everyone who asked. "I don't know what to say. This cannot be happening…"

But the more I said it, the less it mattered. It *was* happening.

My marriage was ending.

"I wonder why they're this close," I said.

"Sit down, away from the window."

I did. "I should go."

"What—why? It's still early."

"It's almost eleven."

"Don't go," Susan said. "Do you want me to change the music? Here, I'll stop knitting. What's wrong?"

"I don't know—"

The room jumped. Books catapulted from their shelves, and the window exploded in a glittery haze. Dust and hot air rolled through the room. I grabbed Susan.

"I'm fine," she said. "Fine."

"My earlink…" I wasn't wearing it.

"On the table."

The music stopped, the lights went out, and an alarm blared on the street outside. Why was my earlink on the table? I found it, pressed it into my right ear and called Margie. Nothing happened. Gunfire rattled in the near-distance, and thunder rumbled—that wasn't thunder. People were shouting in the hall.

"I have to go," I said. "I've made a mistake."

"What?" Susan followed me to the door. "A *mistake*?" She stopped me at the apartment door. "What do you mean a—oh no, your earlink…"

I unlocked the door. In the hall, a stocky Russian was telling everyone to stay indoors. People with flashlights and candles watched from their doorways.

"What's wrong?" I asked Susan. "My earlink .. ?"

"You left it last night, and your wife called."

I felt the blood leave my face. "You . . ."

"I'm sorry."

"You answered it?"

"I didn't think—she called a few hours ago, just before you got here."

I stared at her.

"To stay inside," the Russian was shouting. "Please, everyone to stay inside."

"What's going on?" someone shouted.

"I don't know, but police to tell me to keep all tenants inside."

I told Susan, "I have to go." And stepped into the hall.

"Still not safe outside," the Russian said.

"My window," Susan said, "don't go—my window's broken."

I pressed past the Russian landlord and out the front door. Across the street, people had gathered on the dark sidewalk to watch their apartment buildings burn. All the streetlamps were out, but in the orange-shadow firelight, I could see their faces. Where are the fire crews? I tried my earlink again, stumbled to the sidewalk. It's over with Susan, I told myself. No more—I can't do this anymore. I'll apologize, do whatever it takes. A pick-up truck full of men in ski masks with assault rifles roared past. Helicopters droned in the distance. Our condo was only six blocks away.

The east-west lanes of Fullerton were empty—in the distance, red and blue lights pulsed.

"Hey, where you going?" I didn't slow, and footsteps hurried behind me. "Why you running? You afraid? Stop!"

I froze, and men in ski masks and lumpy body armor jogged closer. The leader pointed a handgun at me. The others were armed with golf clubs and hunting knives.

"Why you out here? You a cop?" the leader asked.

"I'm going home," I said.

"Yeah? Where you live?"

I nodded toward the distant police lights. "That way."

"You get a letter?"

"Yes."

He laughed, and the others edged closer.

"Some balls on you, eh? You saved—ain't random. Ain't nothing random about it."

"You're right, it's not," I said. "I cure diseases—I'm the one who talked to the S-Virus, that's why I have a place in New Jerusalem. They put me ahead of the lottery."

He stared at me, and one of the others muttered in a language I couldn't understand.

"Yeah?" the leader said at last. "Think I shoot you, eh? How about that—you like that?" He jabbed the gun toward my heart.

"I'm sorry," I said. Something exploded behind me—I saw the heat-blast out of the corner of my vision. "I don't choose who gets to…"

"Shut up."

He shot me in the chest.

I jerked back, hit a wall, and slumped to the sidewalk. They laughed, and one swung a golf club at my head, stopped an inch from my eye when I didn't flinch. I felt warmth soaking my shirt, down my belly. The pain came gradually. Talking loudly, the men left. I pawed my shirt. It was too dark to see the blood, but I could taste it. I coughed.

Fuck.

A fire started in my ribs, and I palmed the bricks, found a handhold, dragged my heavy legs. My feet were tingly, I couldn't feel my toes. I planted one foot, found a second hand-hold and strained, pulled myself up, heaving, on the wall. It was slick. Okay. The pain was getting worse. I started to walk and fell hard, yelping as I collapsed. No. I panted, crawled, hauled myself up, coughed blood, and fell again. Then a third time, and finally, my vision spotting, the world blurry with distant shouting, smoke, and gunfire, I hobbled to the edge of the building, staggered to the next wall and kept moving. If I stopped, if I lost the momentum, I would fall. Keep going.

When I started up the stairs of our townhouse, Margie opened the front door. "I can't believe you would come back here. I called you, Jack. *I talked to her.*"

I grabbed the banister, tried to speak and dribbled blood. A police sedan screamed past.

"You…Jack?"

I nodded, vomited blood.

"Oh my God." She came to me. "Come inside—no, we have to go to the hospital. Stay right there, let me get the keys. They didn't break into the car, I just checked." When she came back out, the door banged open, and Calvin charged past her onto the front porch. We never let him outside without his leash. "Calvin!" He hit the sidewalk and kept running. Margie screamed, *"Calvin! No! Come back here right now!"* Tears on her cheeks, I thought for a moment she might drop me to chase the dog. Finally, she grabbed my arm instead. "I can't believe him—he has to come back…"

Calvin was long gone.

My arm slung over her shoulder, we stumbled down the sidewalk to our car. She lowered me onto the passenger seat.

"I hate you," Margie said and started the engine. "I wish we could find the virus that makes *you* do what you do. I'm sorry. Goddamn Calvin, that stupid dog. You'll be fine, it doesn't look that bad. I'm sure you'll be fine."

I rasped, "Then it has to be done over again."

She burst into nervous laughter and drove faster. "God, I wish I never met you."

⚬

I followed Susan off the plane and stared at my reflection in the glass of a vending machine. Margie never saw her dog again.

"Don't look so morose," Susan said. "You want me to buy you a candy bar?"

"You can go," I said.

"What?"

"I don't want to go anymore."

Susan started shaking her head. "Stop it, we made this agreement, you said we would go and live together, and when everyone dies—what's the matter with you? Why are you always like this?"

"I just don't want to do this anymore, it's not fair."

"*Fair?* This from the man who screws around on his wife." I started to walk away, and she called, "You'll change your mind tonight. Jack! Stop it, don't… Jack, please!"

Van Gogh was right.

I took a taxi to Margie's house—I'd given her my mother's old house after Chicago—but no one answered the doorbell, and as I frowned and shuffled in the gray drizzle…wouldn't it be justice if she *wasn't* here, if I collapsed on the steps of my ex-wife's porch, alone…when the door opened. Margie looked older, too thin in a semi-transparent blouse and formal pants. I opened my mouth, she shifted her weight. I shut my mouth again.

"I'm not going to New Jerusalem," I said.

"Why not?"

"I don't love her."

Margie smiled. "Don't say you love *me*. I'm sorry, I shouldn't laugh, it's just—it's been almost a year. The divorce papers, I'm sorry that took so long." She looked away, clenched her jaw, smiled again. "Well. Today is the day, isn't it?"

"Yes, the virus …"

"There is no virus," she said. "How could there be a virus—how could a virus stop our hearts like that? It's *people* doing this, it has to be. Crazy people who want to start over. Either way, it doesn't matter."

That was impossible, but I played along. "If it's just people, maybe they won't do it. Maybe something will go wrong."

She watched the light rain. "Yeah, maybe. What do you want, Jack?"

"I want to die with you."

She swallowed, squeezed the door handle and willed back tears. Everyone who hadn't made it into the lottery, we believed—of course, we hadn't been *officially* told—everyone outside New Jerusalem would die tonight at 12:55 am sharp Eastern Time. It was surreal. Maybe we wouldn't. Maybe she was right, and it wasn't a virus—maybe. It didn't matter why anymore. I just wanted to hold Margie.

"No."

I felt a cold tumor in my stomach. "Please—"

"No," she said again. "I'm sorry. I've planned everything—no, you'll have to be somewhere else. You have Van Gogh to keep you company, don't you?" I tensed, and she said, "I am sorry, though."

"What can I do?"

"Nothing," Margie said. "It's been too long. I'll see you on the other side, Jack." And she shut the door.

Van Gogh loved colors, not black, only rarely black—only at the end: lonely figures in a cemetery-forest and a storm of crows. I understood why. He knew what was coming. Of course he did. I touched my chest, as I turned to walk away. What had been thinking when he raised the pistol? It would have been in French, I thought. I don't speak French.

www.ingramcontent.com/pod-product-compliance
Lightning Source LLC
Chambersburg PA
CBHW061818190726
48289CB00007B/2243